BORROWED MAGIC

WITCH'S BITE SERIES BOOK ONE

STEPHANIE FOXE

STEEL FOX MEDIA LLC

COPYRIGHT

Witch's Bite ©
Borrowed Magic ©
All rights reserved.

Cover Design by Melody Simmons
https://ebookindiecovers.com

Dreams do come true.

CONTENTS

I'm the only healer in two hundred miles that would let a vampire dump a half-dead snack off on my doorstep. I'm also the weakest healer in over two hundred miles, my magical talent is in brewing potions and salves, but I can keep a necker alive if a vampire gets a little overzealous.

Which is why I'm opening the door to a half-dead woman who's bleeding out slowly on my front porch. Her neck is torn in two narrow strips from where they dragged a vampire off of her.

I drop to my knees and put my hand over her heart to take her pulse. It's beating, but thready, and her skin is cold. I grab my X-ACTO knife from right inside the doorway and cut off her top. The poor girl isn't even wearing a bra. Glancing down at her clothes I realize that makes sense; she isn't exactly dressed for church, and any bra would have shown in that shirt.

I run my hands slowly and firmly down her torso, increasing blood production and warming her. Her heart beat regains some confidence as my magic wraps around it. It's moving under my skin like I've pulled it inside me.

I hook my hands under her arms and drag her inside. She's fairly light, so I take a deep breath, then haul her torso up onto the table. Her legs go up next, then I roll her onto her back, but give up on trying to get her on there straight. I could use some help just for this part.

The emergency supplies are all laid out. The IV, scissors, gauze, and cleaning supplies. The IV bag is already hanging from the stand, ready to go. I don't bother with gloves, but I do grab an alcohol wipe and scrub down her arm. The healing goes much smoother the sooner I can get fluids into the injured person.

A vein is easy to find, thankfully, and I slip the needle in carefully. This part has always made my stomach churn. I wish I could heal without all of this, but I'm simply too weak to rely on magic alone.

Now that the IV is started I can continue healing. Her body is sucking up the fluids like a sponge as I push my magic through her, encouraging her body to replenish the blood she lost. They had gotten her to me just in time. She had been very close to beyond my ability to help. I suspect she was fed on by several vampires; there are bites in various places on her torso. If she had already lost quite a bit of blood; having a young vampire lose control while feeding was very risky. The past six months worth of practice I have had pay off for her, maybe working for the vampires isn't a total waste.

I had been contacted by a vampire about six months ago when I was a little desperate for money, working as a waitress doesn't pay quite enough to live off of, and offered a job. The job was simple; I would do house calls to keep the humans they fed on healthy and help them recover more quickly so the vampires could drink from them more often. The vampires bring them to me if there is ever an 'unfortunate incident', which is a professional sounding term for somebody losing control and nearly draining a necker. In return, I'm paid a decent salary, definitely more than I could get paid for my mediocre healing anywhere else.

Healers are rare, good healers even more so, and you almost can't find a healer that'd stoop to help vampire leftovers. We can get a bit snooty since we're a rare breed. Of course, I'm so far at the bottom of the barrel I'm barely even recognized as a healer. I've never been able to earn money from healing before. That's enough to take the snootiness out of anyone.

The vampires also aren't as terrible as I expected. They seem to take care of the people they feed on very well; I think they care about them, possibly even love some of them. It's more of a balanced relationship than I had imagined. I should know better than to buy into stereotypes.

I measure out a small amount of my most used salve.

It will heal the nasty tears on her neck in a matter of days.

"Who the fuck are you?" The girl slurs as she tries to slide off the table. They always wake up faster than I want them to. I think the magic is stimulating.

"Nope, get back on the table, I'm not done yet," I say as I grab her arm. She pulls against my grip with a shaking arm.

"You can't tell me what to do, bitch," she says as she leans forward to try to bite me.

I do not understand why they always try to bite; it's like they forget they're the food and not the vampires. I smack her across the face, hard, and she jerks back, looking at me with wide eyes that are a little more awake.

"Sit the fuck down. Whoever you were playing with almost killed you. I'm in charge of fixing you. If you give me trouble, they will kick your ass," I snap, pointing at a sign hanging on the wall behind me.

It's a simple sign, something I requested after the first few gave me trouble since they were waking up in a strange place with no idea who I was. It says COOP-ERATE OR BE PUNISHED. Beneath the words are the clan's sigil and the clan leader's signature.

The girl's eyes go wide, and she slumps back down on the table.

"Sorry, lady."

"Drink this," I say, handing her a small vial. "It's

gonna be disgusting but don't you dare spit any of it out. It's expensive."

The girl pinches her nose and chokes it down, cursing me and the vampires as soon as she can get a breath. "What the hell was that?"

"Something to replenish your iron and blood levels. You'll probably have a headache until it wears off in a few days, and you'll have a hard time getting drunk."

"I'm supposed to go to a party tonight!"

"Guess you can be the designated driver," I say with a shrug. "Lay down."

She complies, still grumbling about her party. I push her chin to the side and spread the salve on the bites. She yelps and the skin twitches as the area reddens.

She reaches up to scratch it, and I bat her hand away.

"It itches!"

"I know, it's going to itch until it's healed, but if you scratch it, you'll tear it open and then no one is going to want to bite your ugly neck."

She sticks her hands under her arms, looking mutinous, but still complying. I grab one more potion off my desk and hand it to her.

"If you are going to let someone feed on you again within the next 72 hours, take this about an hour before."

She slips it into her pocket, but the pout doesn't leave her face. I toss a plain white t-shirt at her as well, and she pulls it on. My phone buzzes, it's a text from the chauffeur service the vampires arranged.

"Your ride is here, you can leave through that door," I say pointing at the door behind her. I made sure to set up this room so that no one would have to walk through my house to get out. The neckers had a tendency to take things when you weren't looking. After my third patient, a six-foot-tall man had stolen my flip flops I made some changes.

I rub a hand down my face, I'm tired, but healing always gets my adrenaline going. There's no chance I'll fall back asleep now, which is fine since there's order that I need to deliver, I glance at the time again, today. I have just enough time to make it and deliver it before lunch.

I've been brewing since I was five; so I could make any of these potions in my sleep. The process is cathartic these days. Brewing has always given me a sense of control. It's measured, predictable, and reliable. Water boils at the same temperature every time. A bat eye, dandelion petals, and a pinch of fool's gold always brews into a simple blood replenishing potion.

Mr. Bronson, god rest his soul, had never understood that. He thought the brewing was what got me in with a bad crowd, but it was what had kept me from really losing myself. It was helping me get my feet back on the ground now too.

I wipe a drop of sweat from my forehead and lean over to crank up the window unit. This old rental house doesn't seem to have any insulation left, and Texas is hot as Satan's balls in the summer. If I didn't have the contract with the vampires, I'd be moving into one of the little apartments in town instead of renewing the lease on this place, but I need the privacy.

Soon enough I forget about the heat and vampires and even Mr. Bronson's voice in the back of my head telling me I ought not do the devil's work. I've been working on this acne salve for two weeks. Each stage has to sit undisturbed in the cauldron for thirty-six hours. Then I had to wait for it to settle into the right consistency. It's been stubborn, to say the least.

I lift the lid from the cauldron and poke at the translucent, rosy substance. It's slick and about the same thickness as lard.

"Finally," I lean down and give it a quick sniff too. It smells like rose and marshmallow.

I scoop it into little plastic tubs, wipe off any drips, and slap the labels that Maybelle printed for me on them. It says 'Carter's Brews' in a swirly blue font over a shiny, silver background. It's a little girly for me, but she said it was great marketing and since Maybelle runs the most successful business in town, I took her advice without arguing.

The next brew is a quicker one; there is no need to rest it. It actually works best the faster I can get it bottled. It's been one of the best sellers which suits me just fine. The centering brew is simple and cheap to make. It was one of my mother's best sellers, but that's to be expected in a big town. I wasn't sure how it would do here. Apparently, even out in the country, people want the pinpoint focus and energy the potion provides. They're willing to deal with the minor headache it causes, and I can't blame them. As far as side effects that's not half bad.

The cauldron I need isn't where it should be. I turn in a circle, scanning the room, then remember the one I need is still sitting by the sink. I'd left a potion too long the other day and have been scrubbing goo off it since.

The cauldron is sparkling, polished steel. I bought it two months ago when the previous one fell apart. The magic puts quite a bit of stress on the metal.

I twist the knob on the stove and the burner flares to life. Before the metal of the cauldron gets too hot, I dip my finger in the saltwater solution I keep next to the stove and trace a spiral from the middle of the cauldron up and around the sides to the top edge.

The ingredients for the brew are all lined up on the shelf behind the stove. I set a plain, clear crystal the size of a pea in the very center of the spiral and pour essence of mint over the top. The mint obediently settles into the lines I drew in the bottom of the cauldron, slowly creeping up the sides as though it's trying to escape the heat.

I pull a bottle of cheap Prosecco out of the mini fridge and pour it straight into the cauldron. Something bubbly to give them pep while the mint makes them sharp. It hisses up immediately begins to boil.

I pick out a few wasp wings and crumple them in my hand as I grab my sturdy, old wooden stirring rod. They drop into the cauldron, and I stir quickly. Right, right, left, right, right, left. I continue until the rhythm feels natural and mindless.

The mint, still clinging to the sides of the cauldron, begins to glow green as the brew tugs at it. I pass my hand over the cauldron, my fingers wiggling and scattering bright sparks into the bubbling liquid.

"There we go," I whisper as the brew begins to spin on its own. I lift the stirring rod out of it, and roiling liquid begins to spin faster and faster until it suddenly stills in a flash of green tinted light. "One down, six to go."

The hours pass quickly as I fill little glass vials with my potions, then start another batch. One of these days I'll be able to afford a bigger cauldron.

I'm a sweaty, tired mess by the time I'm done. The workroom is scattered with ingredients, and I need to wash out this cauldron, but I'm actually running out of time to get to town.

I double check my order list and make sure everything is packed up and ready to put in the car, then head into the central part of the house to take a quick shower. I can't show up to Maybelle's looking like a hobo.

A country song twangs out of my speakers as I pull into town. I wouldn't have been caught dead listening to country music before I moved here, but it's become something of a guilty pleasure. The songs make me nostalgic for a peaceful small town life I've never had.

Maybelle's General Store is the most prominent store on Main Street. The sides of the building facing the road are glass all the way around and lit up day and night with antique styled lanterns that always stay polished to brilliance. Nobody can walk by without slowing down to look inside.

She has everything from clothes to kitchenware to potions. Upstairs is a cafe with a balcony that overlooks the street. I can smell the pies from down the street near the service entrance where I'm parking.

Johnny is at my trunk before I can get out of my car. That man has a sixth sense for deliveries.

"Hey Johnny, how's it hanging?"

"Little to the left," he says with a cackle as he grabs the first box of potions out of my trunk. Johnny is missing a few teeth and has spent so much time under the sun that he's darker than even Mr. Brunson was. Johnny's wrinkles are more like craters, even though I suspect he's only about sixty. He moves too fast to be any older. I follow him inside and set my box down on a table in the storeroom, the little vials all clinking together.

"Is that who I think it is?" Maybelle comes out of her office in a whirl of color. She's wearing a ruffled pink skirt with an exquisite yellow blouse. A teal headscarf is holding her curly red hair out of her face, which is covered in freckles and brightened by a wide smile.

She's even older than Johnny, but nobody would dare mention it.

"My sweet Olivia, I have not seen you in a full week!" She says as she sweeps me into a hug, bending me side to side. I hug back as well as I can. "Have you been avoiding me?"

"Not at all," I laugh as I pull away. "I've just been a little busy this week."

"Busy with that good-for-nothing boy," she says, flicking the tip of my nose before she sashays over to my box of potions and inspects a few.

"He's not that bad. Besides, we aren't even dating. We're just getting to know each other."

"You are having sex with him, and you are thinking about a future with him before you've even gotten him to say he's your boyfriend. You know that's backward."

I shrug and look at the floor. She's old-fashioned, and it never does much good to argue with her. It had been over a year since I'd gotten laid. Tyler was easy on the eyes and had that good ol' boy feel about him. He opened the door and paid for our dates and always made sure I came first.

"It's good enough for now Maybelle."

She tisks at me but drops it. "I have a new business proposition for you since you're here."

I perk up immediately. "What is it?"

"I bought a little storefront down the street a few months ago. I think I want to turn it into an apothecary.

What would you think about supplying me with more medicinal brews?"

Medicinal brews cost five to ten times as much as other brews. They're tricky to brew, tricky enough that people won't buy them from anyone other than a healer's guild shop. Unless they're stupid. I can brew them, but I'd never be able to sell them on my own. Maybelle however—people would buy it from her.

"I think I would like to do that very much," I say, hoping she can't tell there's a lump in my throat. If I had a contract like that it would change everything. I wouldn't have to work for the vampires. I would be able to afford a rent house that wasn't a hundred years old with rats living under the porch.

Maybelle nods at me with a twinkle in her eye.

"I have contractors coming tomorrow to start building it out. I'll let you know when I'll need some brews. You better give me your best work girly."

"You know I don't do anything else."

She nods proudly. "You coming upstairs for some pie?"

"Not today," I say standing up straight and smoothing down my shirt. "Apparently I need to go visit Gerard."

"Alright, well you don't be a stranger. I better see you again in a few days."

"I promise I'll come by," I say, pecking her on the cheek and heading towards the door.

"If you don't I'll send Johnny to grab you. Don't think I won't!"

"Wouldn't doubt it for a second!" I say as I slip back out into the heat.

I climb into my car and let out a sigh. I'm ecstatic about the business opportunity, but medicinal brews mean specialty ingredients. And specialty ingredients mean Gerard. And Gerard is creepy. There's no use putting it off though.

A quick five-minute drive brings me to Gerard's warehouse. It's the polar opposite of Maybelle's place. His office is in a rickety metal storefront with one window that is boarded up with weathered plywood. The door is always locked, and the sign on the door reads closed. I've never been sure how he makes a living since I've never seen another person here.

I take a deep breath and rap out three loud knocks on the thick metal door, wait three seconds, then one more. I step back from the door and settle in for a wait. He always makes me wait at least five minutes, which is why I jump when the door immediately swings inward.

Gerard is in the doorway, eyes wide and bloodshot. His white t-shirt is stained, and he is sweatier than usual.

"Get inside," he whispers hoarsely, scuttling backward out of the sunlight.

I leap inside to get in before he pulls the door shut on me. It's almost pitch black, so I pull out my phone and use the light from the screen to follow him back to his makeshift office, stepping around moldy pallets and trash. There's also a dead rat, but that's better than the live one that ran across my foot the last time I was here. Gerard is practically jogging, and he keeps scratching at his arms.

"Everything okay Gerard?" I ask as I jog to catch up.

He stops and whips around. "Better watch your back, Olivia. There's trouble in town and none of the powers that be are going to do a thing about it. They don't listen to reason."

"What kind of trouble?"

"The bad kind," he says as he steps into his office.

Cryptic as always. The man's impossible to have a coherent conversation with. I put my phone back in my pocket, the ambient glow of eight computer screens is enough to see by. This whole room is a spiderweb of wires across the walls and ceiling. There's a pile of empty ramen containers in one corner and a big water jug next to a black rolling chair that leans to the left. He tosses me a notepad and then a pen which I barely manage to catch.

I write down my order, mentally running through the ingredients for the new brews I'll need to make. Some of them I haven't made in years, but the recipes are ingrained in me. A few minutes pass, then I hand the notepad back, three pages filled out front and back. He flips through it eagerly.

"These are new," he says squinting at me. "Who do

you think you're gonna get to buy healing brews from a girl with a felony on her record?"

"Can you get it all for me or not? I think I'll need to be brewing within a month," I ask, trying not to bristle at his question. There's no way I could do this without Maybelle, but I don't need Gerard of all people reminding me of past mistakes. He's always known things about me he shouldn't.

He squints at me for a moment longer, then nods.

I take that as my cue to leave and start picking my way back through the warehouse.

Right before I reach the door, he yells across the empty space. "Try not to die!"

I open the door and step back into the sunlight, blinking. I have goosebumps despite the heat.

Rudie's is the best bar in town, and also boasts the best hamburger and curly fries in three counties, possibly even the nation. They open at eleven am, except on Sundays when they don't open until two pm and have a dedicated lunch crowd. Every time I've had the money to spare I end up here for lunch.

My stomach growls as I walk inside and the delicious aroma of fried food hits me. It's glorious. Chevy is behind the bar handing over a beer to Fred, one of the regulars. Chevy waves at me before moving down the bar to take the next order. Susan waves too, pointing at a free table in the corner. I nod and take a seat with my back to the wall. It takes a minute before she can make it over to me, stopping at a few tables to accept a request for more water or sweet tea.

"Hey darling, the usual?"

"Yes, ma'am," I say with a grin. It's been almost two weeks since I've been in for a burger and I've been craving them.

"You got it," she says before bustling away.

The door to my right tinkles and I glance up, a smile springing to my face when I see Tyler walk in. The smile turns brittle when I spot Joanna, the blonde bimbo town slut, hanging off his side. She isn't interested unless the guy has a girlfriend or a wife. I've never been sure if it's daddy issues or if she's just mean. He's got his hand on her ass.

He doesn't see me until he gets a solid five steps in. My face is going blank like it does when I get mad. He stops in his tracks, and Joanna trips over his feet. She finally catches on to where he is looking and rolls her eyes.

"Come oooon Tyler. Let's get lunch."

"Just give me a second to talk to Liv, alright?"

Joanna sticks her bottom lip out like a five-year-old and blinks her eyes up at him. "But I'm hungry baby. You wore me out this morning."

So that's why he hadn't responded to my texts since yesterday afternoon.

"I'll be just a minute," he says as he finally gets his arm out of her grip.

She huffs and shoves him. "Fine, go talk to that stupid bitch, but I'm not hanging around waiting for you to talk to some other girl."

She throws a glare my direction and stomps out.

I lean back in my chair as Tyler approaches, rubbing his hand across the back of his neck.

"Hey Liv," he says, looking at me with a half smile.

I stare him down, a hundred useless things running through my mind, like the last time I saw that smile and how his hands felt on my ass.

"Look, we hadn't talked about being exclusive or anything."

I don't say anything; there's no point. We hadn't 'defined the relationship' or whatever, but he'd started talking about taking me to meet his family in a few weeks because they were having a barbecue. It had felt like we were dating. Then again, any guy I chose was almost guaranteed to be an asshole. It was a family curse.

"I must have thought it was implied when you told me no one else had ever made you feel this way and you didn't even want to look at another girl."

"Come on Liv; we were in the middle of, you know," he says, waggling his eyebrows and glancing around like he's embarrassed to say the word sex in public. "That doesn't count for anything."

"Tyler," I say carefully, leaning forward onto my elbows. "Fuck off and let me enjoy my burger."

Susan walks up with perfect timing and sets my burger down with way more force than necessary, bouncing a couple of curly fries off onto the table. I rescue them and shove them all in my mouth at once.

"See ya some other day Tyler," Susan says with her arms crossed and a thicker accent than usual.

"Whatever," he says before storming out of the door he came in.

"I'm gonna bring you a milkshake sweetie."

"No, that's okay Susan, I'll just—"

"No objections allowed. It's on the house, Chevy will insist on it."

She walks away before I can object again, not that I really want to argue. Their milkshakes are great, and I could use some chocolate.

I take a bite of my burger, but it doesn't taste quite as good as it usually does when I'm not trying not to cry in public.

2

M r. Muffins is staring at me from the hallway when I slam the front door behind me.

"Don't look at me like that," I mutter as I stalk into the kitchen. The tequila is in the same cupboard as my glasses. I grab the bottle and take a swig before dropping heavily into a chair at the little two-person table crammed into the space between the kitchen and the living room. I had texted Patrick before I left Rudie's and he still hasn't responded yet. He wasn't a Tyler fan, so I'm sure he'll be excited.

My laptop dings with a new email. It's the deposit from the vampires for the healing I did this morning. I take another drink of tequila and open my account to check the balance. One thousand twenty-two dollars and sixty-five cents. It's the most money I've had in the bank at one time, by legal means at least, but if I can supply the apothecary for Maybelle, this'll be nothing. I'll have thousands.

I grin as I take another drink. Fuck Tyler. This is a celebration.

My resolve lasts for about thirty minutes. My phone rings, a sickeningly romantic country song blaring out of the tinny speakers, Tyler's number flashing on the screen. I reject the call and take a drink, sliding my phone away from me across the table.

I move to the living room and turn on the tv scrolling through the static and news channels trying to find something decent, but all that's on is romantic comedies and telenovelas.

My phone rings again, and I stand up on the couch, taking another, longer, drink from the bottle.

"Muffins! I just thought of a new game! Every time he calls, I drink. You think I'll survive the night?"

Muffins meows and twitches her tail disapprovingly.

Two hours later I'm face down on the bathroom floor since it's the coldest place in the house and the room is spinning even though I'm lying still.

"Men are stupid, Muffins," I roll over to find she is facing the door licking her stomach. "Oh my god are you even listening to me? You know what, you're stupid too."

Muffins stops licking and swishes her tail.

"You heard me," I mutter before sitting up to take another swig from the bottle. My stomach rolls and I grimace as I grab the edge of the toilet.

"I think I drank too much," I moan. "Fucking Tyler and his fucking phone calls."

Muffins crawls into my lap, her claws pricking through my jeans.

"Ow ow ow!"

She rubs her face against my chin as the tears start. I hug her close and just feel sorry for myself.

"This why I keep you around you know," I whisper into her fur.

I blink one eye open, then hear the banging again. I try to sit up quickly, my first thought is that someone is trying to break in, but my head objects strongly to quick movements, and I end up on hands and knees. I'm still in the bathroom, and my mouth tastes like something crawled inside it and died.

"Police, open up! We know you're in there!"

What the fuck. I get my feet underneath me and find my phone. It's almost two pm. I don't have any messages from the vampires, so no one died on my porch last night. I rub my eyes then lean over and take a quick drink from the tap so I can talk a little easier.

I look like shit. My hair is falling out of the ponytail I had it in, and my eyeliner is smudged down my cheek. Whatever.

They bang on my front door again.

"Alright! I'm coming! I'm coming!" I yell, despite my headache.

I jerk the door open, and I'm immediately blinded by the late afternoon sun. I keep all the blinds down in the house, so it's always nice and dark.

There are two men, and one of them flashes me a badge that looks official.

"Whatever, just come inside, it's too damn bright out here," I say opening the door wider and retreating back towards the living room.

The men walk inside. The one that showed me his badge is tall, most likely ripped underneath his clothes, and has a military haircut. He looks me over and raises a thick brow. The other guy I've seen around town before. He's a little shorter, more wiry, and has almost white blonde hair.

"Olivia Carter?"

"The one and only," I say sitting down on the couch. "What do you need?"

"I'm Detective Jason Martinez, and this is Detective Alexander Novak," the taller one says. "Do you know Jessica Johnson?"

"Um," I say, going through people I've met recently in my head. "No, that name doesn't sound familiar at all."

"Do you recognize this woman?" Novak asks, stepping across the living room to shove a picture in my face. There's a young woman with blonde hair and a freshly healed bite on her neck spread out naked on the grass. Her skin is paper white, she's been drained.

I sigh, of course I recognize her.

"Yeah, I recognize her. Just didn't know her name. Early yesterday morning, around four-thirty, she got dropped off. I healed her and sent her away."

Martinez grabs the two chairs from the table and sets them in the living room across from me.

He and Novak sit down.

"Did you see her after that?" Martinez asks sitting down in the chair on the left.

"Nope."

"Are you sure she was alive when she left your house?" Novak asks.

So it's going to be like that. I lean back and cross my arms. "She was definitely alive when she was dropped off on my doorstep and was definitely alive when she walked out the door."

"Take us through what happened from the beginning," Martinez says, pulling out a notepad. Novak has his hands on his knees, one finger tapping restlessly.

"I got a text, just said 'dropping off.' I threw on some clothes, got a few things together, heard them drop her on the front porch. Got out there and fixed her up no problem. Called a car for her and she left."

I was already skirting the line of confidentiality; I definitely wasn't going to tell them she was almost dead. I also wasn't going to let them know I went through the same routine at least twice a month. It had gotten more frequent recently too, but some of the neckers weren't hurt all that bad. It was more like the vampires were getting used to the idea that they could keep their toys in better shape.

"You said 'they' dropped her off, who was it?" Jason asked.

"I don't know, I never see them."

"Why don't you see them? Ask questions about what happened to your patients?" Novak asks, sitting up slightly.

"No need to, it would be a waste of my time. It's always an issue of blood loss, and that's something I can fix easily. If it's beyond my skill level, I'd just call 911 for an ambulance."

"And that's something you've had to do," Martinez pauses, flipping back a page, "three times?"

"Yes."

"Where was she going?" Novak asks.

"I don't know, and I didn't ask because it's none of my business."

"How often do the vampires send people to your door for healing?" Martinez asks as he writes something down in his notepad.

"That's confidential."

Martinez looks up, a frown tugging at his lips.

"Do you want to be charged for impeding an ongoing investigation?" Novak asks, moving his arm so that his sleeve slips upward just enough to show me the coven symbol tattooed on his wrist.

The coven was backing the investigation then, which meant there was something bigger going on than one death. I look at the tense line of Novak's shoulders. Maybe something big enough to spook Gerard.

It's early, and I'm too hungover, for these kinds of threats. Covens are always butting into investigations involving paranormals and getting heavy-handed when it isn't necessary. The council lives and breathes public relations, and every coven wants to be on their good side. Humans can fuck up all they want, but if a paranormal is caught being evil, all hell breaks loose.

"No, but legally you have to have a warrant before I can divulge confidential client information. I'm not getting sued by the vampires. Just come back with a warrant, and I'll tell you whatever you want to know."

"You were the last person to see her alive, are you sure you don't want to help us, Miss Carter?" Novak asks. He's getting heavy handed with his threats now.

"I'll help you find your way out, how about that?" I say standing and pointing at the front door. "I'm sure you have my phone number somewhere, give me a call when you get a warrant, and we can chat all you want."

They both stand reluctantly. Novak's face has gone red from irritation. I briefly wonder how he survives summers in Texas with skin that pale.

Novak heads out the door immediately, but Martinez takes a moment to set his card down on the table.

"In case you change your mind."

"Sure," I say moving the card towards the center of the table. I can throw it away after he leaves.

He opens the door but stops in the doorway, with the sun behind him I can't see his face.

"Why do you work for the vampires? Even when they aren't breaking the law, all they do is hurt people. They prey on the weak."

"For the money," I say. It's a simple answer that isn't really a lie, it's not the whole truth, but I can feel the accusation in his question. He doesn't deserve the truth from me, not when he's come to my house and accused me of murder.

He stays in the doorway for another breath, like I might add onto what I just said, then turns and walks out to his partner who is staring daggers at me from their car.

3

"You will be at the clanhouse in fifteen minutes, or we will find you and drag you there," Emilio hisses into the phone.

Emilio is always so dramatic, he buys into the Victorian, goth vampire persona.

"Oh calm the fuck down, I'm already on my way. I'll be there in five minutes."

Emilio hangs up without responding. I drop my phone into my lap and sigh. I don't want this to fall apart, but I also don't want to get murdered by paranoid vampires. My cross is hung around my neck, I rubbed myself down with holy water right before I left, and I have a few nasty potions on hand just in case.

I've had a lot of time to think after the detectives had left, and I don't like any of the things I've come up with. I doubt anyone hates me enough, much less knows me well enough, to frame me for Jessica's murder. It doesn't make sense for the vampires to have her healed and then kill her either. Not that it was impossible, they could be really damn confusing sometimes.

There was a chance, small though it was, that the coven was involved. They haven't given me any trouble since I moved into town though. They had made it clear I wasn't welcome in their coven, but that hadn't exactly been big news. Covens didn't accept fuckups.

I don't really know any of the weres in this town. I've seen them around but the alpha, whoever they are, keeps everyone in line and out of the public eye.

No, whatever was going on had to be about the vampires. Maybe whoever had gotten pulled off Jessica that night had gone back for the rest the next night when they woke up. They could get fixated like that sometimes. My shoulder aches just thinking about it.

I turn down the long driveway. The house looms over the yard like an old ghost. The vampires had bought a plantation style house fifty or sixty years ago. The inside is modernized, but the outside is all over-grown vines and boarded up windows. It looks like it's haunted.

I park by one of their sleek black limos and climb out as the sun sets on the horizon. The door is already swinging open. Emilio is hovering in the shadows watching me.

"Good morning, Emilio," I say quietly as I walk inside.

He slams the door shut behind me and looks down

his nose as he adjusts his lace cuffs. He speaks with a slight hiss, "You know it issn't morning, and you know that joke iss never funny."

I look behind me but don't see Patrick creeping up. I frown, this is typically when he pops up to tell Emilio his sense of humor is dead or something like that. Which is why Patrick is my favorite. He had scared me the first few times I was here; he thought it was hilarious to sneak up behind me and try to get me to scream. He had finally succeeded the third time he tried. He had broken down laughing so hard he cried. I had ended up on the floor with him, laughing harder than I had in years. We've been best buds ever since. He's the only vampire I'd ever go to a bar with, and he's the only one other than Javier and Emilio with my cell number.

"Where's Patrick?"

"Javier is eager to speak with you, follow me," Emilio says, completely ignoring my question, as usual.

The house is always dark inside. The only lighting is soft, blue-tinted LEDs built into the baseboards every few feet. At first the darkness it put me on edge, but since I've been coming every two weeks for six months, I've gotten used to it. Patrick explained that it really was more for comfort anyhow, it just had the added effect of scaring newcomers. Blood tastes better when it's pumping faster, apparently.

Actual light is coming from under the door to Javier's room though. He uses his bedroom as an office.

Emilio knocks once, then pulls the door open, waving me inside.

Javier is lanky, but always well groomed unlike some of his clan. He's wearing a crisp, white button-down shirt, unbuttoned and hung loosely, over black slacks. His dark skin is dampened by his ghostly pallor causing a stark contrast to his black hair. He is standing in front of his window with the thick, red curtains tied back so he can watch the moon rise.

He turns around, looking me up and down with relish.

"You cut your hair," he comments.

My hand goes to it automatically. It had been down almost to my waist, I cut it to my shoulders about a week ago, and I'm still getting used to it.

"It's hot outside," I say with a shrug.

He pushes out his bottom lip in a pout. "It's still lovely, but I did always hope to see all that hair fanned out on my pillow."

I roll my eyes. "The police came to my house today, the necker you dropped off the night before last ended up dead."

He sits back on the window ledge. "So I heard. What did you tell the police?"

"That I fixed her up, she left alive, and that if they wanted to know more, they had to come back with a warrant."

Javier chuckles, a deep sound that always makes my skin crawl. "How did they take that?"

"One of the detectives is a witch, he flashed his coven mark," I say with a shrug. "I'm guessing they will come back with a warrant if they can."

Javier stands and grabbed an envelope from the bookshelf to his left and tosses it at me. I catch it just before it hits my face and scowl at him.

"What's this?"

"Your six-month bonus, we always want our employees to feel appreciated," Javier says spreading his arms wide and grinning with a mouth full of teeth that are unnaturally sharp.

So, it was encouragement to keep my mouth shut, possibly even if there was a warrant. The smile, however, is a threat.

"Always good to be appreciated, Javier," I say as I slip the envelope into my back pocket. "I'll let you know if they contact me again."

"Please do, you will have our protection if they harass you of course."

I nod my head politely and move towards the door before I pause. "Do you have any idea what might have Gerard spooked?"

Javier's jaw twitches. "No, I didn't realize he was spooked. Did he say something to you?"

"He just suggested that I try not to die."

"Death isn't so bad," Javier says with a wink.

"See you next week for check-ups," I say as I slip out the door. He knows something. Familiar anger is bubbling up in my stomach. Secrets always end up getting the peons hurt, and lord knows I'm definitely a peon.

I flip through the contents of the envelope as I walk down the hall to Patrick's room, five hundred, not bad. I knock on Patrick's door. When there's no answer I try the handle, it's unlocked. The door swings open soundlessly, and I flick on the lights. The room is empty, but nothing is out of place. The sheets on the bed are rumpled, and there's a blood stain on the pillow. All normal for Patrick, he's a messy eater. The only thing that's odd is that he isn't here.

I turn the light off and shut the door behind me, unease settling over me.

It's ten pm, and I've called Patrick's cell about eight times. When I find him, I'm going to kick his ass. It's been about a week since I've heard from him. I thought maybe he was mad at me for that comment I made about how he's been kind of slutty lately, which I meant as a joke, but he took personally for some reason. The longest he's ever gone without talking to me before this is maybe two days, it's gone beyond weird at this point.

I can't sit at the house anymore. There's a small chance that if he's just out wandering around that he'll be in town tonight. He loves Rudie's, there's always a ton of humans there to mess with, and girls that want to feel a little dangerous by flirting with a vampire. It's somewhere to start at least.

I grab my best jeans out of my closet and pull them on. I don't have much in the way of boobs, no more than a handful, but I make up for it in ass. The jeans definitely show that off to good advantage. I grab a silky, dark red blouse too. It's low cut, and one of only two nice shirts I have.

I never know what to do with my hair, so it just hangs straight around my face. I touch up my eyeliner and mascara and shrug at the mirror. It'll do for tonight.

The drive into town feels like it takes twice as long as usual. I have the music cranked up loud, my fingers tapping out an unsteady rhythm on the steering wheel. The parking lot is filling up when I pull in; I have to park towards the back where the lights just barely reach.

I walk in through the back entrance and head towards the bar. The music is loud, country music still, they don't switch to hip-hop until after midnight. There's a big group of guys in the corner, eyes glued to the tv watching some kind of MMA fight. The bar itself is three people deep waiting for drinks. Chevy is back there with the other bartenders, including a girl I don't recognize that must be new.

I wind my way through the crowd and get in line. The thought of alcohol makes my stomach churn, but I need at least a beer, so I'm not standing around without anything in my hands. I finally make it up to the bar after a few minutes, and Chevy nods in greeting.

"What can I get you?" He shouts over the music.

"Beer, you got anything new in?"

"I've got a new pecan porter."

"I'll try that. Hey, have you seen Patrick around since last night?"

"Nope, but if I see him, I'll tell him you're looking for him," he says as he grabs a glass, spinning it twice before filling it to the brim with the dark, foamy liquid.

"Thanks, Chevy."

He waits for me to taste it before he goes to help the next person. I take a long drink, my eyes shutting on their own. It's sweet and a little nutty and wonderfully refreshing. I'm definitely going to have to order this again. I give Chevy a thumbs up.

There aren't any tables open, so I push back through the crowd and find an empty space along the wall where I can watch for Patrick.

Most of the faces look familiar, some because I've healed them and others just because they're always at Rudie's. One of the familiar ones is attached to a girl named Dawn. She looks like she's already a little drunk as she stumbles towards me with a distraught look on her face.

"Olivia," she says as she grabs my arm, making my porter splash over onto my knuckles. I push her back gently, but firmly.

"Don't spill my beer, Dawn."

"Oh sorry," she says, her face screwing up and her lip trembling.

"Look, it's okay, what'd you want?" I really don't want her to start crying. She can go for hours once she gets started.

"You seen Britney around? Like with the vampires or whatever?"

"You know I don't talk about what I do or don't see with the vampires."

She sighs and smears the back of her hand across her nose, sniffling. "I know it's just she's been missing for a few days, and I'm worried, okay?"

Another missing person. I believe in a lot of things. That people are inherently evil; Maybelle is an exception to that rule, and that curly fries are the best fries. One thing I don't believe in is coincidences.

"How long has she been missing?"

"Since like two weeks ago. She was supposed to come hang last week, like, she promised. She wanted to get together with Bryan, and she wouldn't just not show up, you know?"

"Maybe she found herself a vampire or something?" I say, trying to reassure her even though in my gut I know she's right to be worried.

"I guess," Dawn attempts a smile.

A hand waving frantically catches my attention. Tyler is pushing his way through the crowd headed straight for me.

"I gotta go. I hope you find your friend," I say, chugging down the rest of my porter and shoving the empty glass in Dawn's hand. She looks confused and almost drops it. I'll look for Patrick some other night.

I'm two steps from the door when a hand closes around my arm. I turn around to snap at Tyler, but the person grabbing me is a woman. Her nails press into my skin, and her ruby red lips are twisted into a sneer.

"Why don't we walk together?" she asks.

I glance at her wrist, it has the same coven mark as the detective. Shit.

"Nah, you can go ahead without me," I say as I attempt to tug my arm out of her grip.

A large, bald man steps up behind her, jacket parted just enough to show me a gun. The gun is probably the least scary thing he has.

I can go with them now while we're in at least a semi-public place, or I can give them the slip and have them show up at my house for a much more tense conversation later. I might be able to hold them off there, but I'm not sure I want to bet my life on it.

I catch Chevy's eye at the bar; he's cleaning a glass very slowly, watching what's going down. At least someone will know where to point the police if I disappear tonight.

"Fine, lead the way."

The woman tightens her grip on my arm and drags me out the door. The bald man follows close behind. Her heeled boots clunk heavily against the wood of the patio, a few people look up as we pass, but they're too absorbed in their own conversations to notice the tension.

"So, are y'all here to recruit me for your coven? Heard about how awesome I was and just couldn't wait?" I ask as we pass the first row of cars and the lights from the bar fade.

Scarlett, the nickname seems fitting, rolls her eyes. The prick of her nails on my skin makes me itch to do something stupid, but I know it's not worth it.

We stop in front of a black car with tinted windows and my heartbeat kicks into overdrive.

"Get in," Baldy rumbles from behind me.

I twist and yank my arm, stepping away from Scarlett.

"I'm not getting in that car. If you two want to talk, you can do it here."

Leaving the bar was a courtesy to Chevy, and if I'm honest, bought me some time to think. I know deep down in my soul that if I get in that car, I'll disappear permanently.

Scarlett snaps her fingers, and a flame wraps around her fingers and down her hand.

"Get in the car, or I'll make you," she says with a smile, her eyes glinting red from the light of the flame. Fire witches always think they're hot shit. Most of them have no idea how to use the magic to its fullest potential.

I pull a thin vial out of my back pocket.

"I guarantee your coven doesn't have an antidote for this," I say as I wiggle it in their faces. "Whatever message you have for me can be given to me right here, right now."

Baldy is watching the vial, his hand twitching like he thinks he might be fast enough to grab it before I can break it.

I put a little pressure on the vial, just enough for the glass to give a little.

Baldy's jaw tenses and he glances at Scarlett. She purses her lips and sighs, extinguishing the flame.

"You need to tell the police that Javier is the one draining the girls that have been disappearing," Scarlett says. "You can tell them you were just too afraid to come forward before."

Girls. How many have disappeared? Jessica. Britney. I haven't been paying attention to the news lately.

"Do you have proof Javier is the one draining them?" I say, hoping my concern doesn't show on my face. Javier would never risk his little kingdom just to drain some neckers.

"No, but that doesn't matter, and you know it. Javier is responsible for every vampire in this district," Scarlett says, her voice snapping in irritation.

"So you want to pin it on him and what? Just hope the murders stop?"

"The vampires got sloppy and killed them, Carter, there's nothing more to it than that. This needs to be settled quickly and quietly, you know the rules."

"Is the council already looking into this?"

"No," Baldy says, stepping a little closer to me. "And

this will be resolved before they do. This district has a perfect record, and we will not allow the vampires to mar that."

Gerard's warning is ringing in my ears. He said that trouble had come to town, but the vampires have been here for over a hundred years. Something else is going on.

"You've got a witch in the damn police, why do you need me to lie?"

"He still needs evidence!" Scarlett shouts. "We have to work through the human's legal system, as you well know."

"You are not leaving here tonight until you give us your word that you will do as instructed. You will call Detective Novak tomorrow morning at eight am and let him know that you do have information and that you'd like to speak with him right away. If you do not cooperate, you will face punishment by the coven," Baldy says in an even tone.

By punishment he means death. Covens are fucking overbearing.

"Like hell, I will," I say throwing the vial onto the ground. I'm already running, eyes screwed tightly shut, as it explodes in a flash of light and a boom that rattles everything around us. Through the ringing in my ears, I can hear car alarms going off. I open my eyes and pull another vial out of my pocket, this one is a little nastier, and I hope I don't have to use it.

4

I crouch down behind a row of cars, running as fast I can in such an awkward position. I can hear Scarlett screeching something, but Baldy is silent. He scares me a little more, especially since I don't know what he can do.

I stop by a big truck and crouch behind one of the tires. I can see my car, but it's in a different row. I'll have to go out into the open. I should have brought another flash-bang potion.

There is the distinct crunch of gravel behind me. I run without even looking and hear the footsteps speed up behind me. I skid to a stop behind my car and turn and throw the second vial. I don't want to be too close when it breaks.

Baldy is directly in its path, his skin a mottled, dark gray. I grin, impervs are always more caught off guard by this kind of potion. They tend to think they're actually invincible. The vial breaks on his chest as he barrels towards me.

I don't even see Scarlett until the bright light of a fireball comes hurtling towards me from behind Baldy. Baldy clutches his chest, his mouth gaping uselessly as he falls to his knees. The fireball fizzles out of existence, and Scarlett hits her knees behind him, her mouth open in a silent scream.

I yank my car door open and jump inside. The two seconds it takes to turn the car on and get it in reverse feel like a century. I only have five more seconds before they get their oxygen back. I back out, car swinging a foot from Baldy's head.

My tires spin and kick up gravel as I shift into first. Scarlett's indignant scream is the only warning I get before a fireball engulfs my car from back to front. Bathing the thing in a fire resistance potion was a pain in my ass, but I don't regret a second of it now. The fire is still hot enough that it probably singed the paint, but I'll worry about that later.

I pull out onto the main road, my tires screeching on the pavement. I make a beeline for my house. Since I didn't actually injure anyone, the coven probably won't show up at my home in force to kill me tonight. They seem to want me alive for now at least.

My knuckles are white on the steering wheel. I'm already starting to shake. I hate this feeling after a fight when my body doesn't realize the danger has passed.

I glance at the rearview mirror every few seconds.

The roads outside of town are always empty. It would be noticeable if someone followed me.

The house looks perfectly innocent as I drive up the driveway. The light in the kitchen is still on, and there are no black cars waiting for me. I step out of the vehicle hesitantly, every sense on high alert.

I crack open the back door and listen carefully for the telltale creak of the floor, or a breath. I step inside and shut the door behind me, turning the lock.

Something touches my leg, and I scream, throwing the lights on as I scramble for a potion on the workbench.

Muffins stares up at me, not pleased with the ruckus I just made at all.

"You fucking, stupid, worthless cat. Trying to kill me," I gasp out as I slide to the floor. "Swear to god I'll take you to the pound if you ever do that again."

She meows and walks away with her tail held high.

I rub my hands briskly over my face and stand up. With the adrenaline fading, I'd like nothing more than to just go to bed, but I'm alone, and I can't risk letting the coven walk up to my house and murder me in my sleep.

Mr. Brunson wouldn't approve of what I'm about to do. Honestly, my mother wouldn't either.

"There's a balance Livvy, especially with brewing. You give yourself a high, be prepared for the low."

I slam my copper cauldron down on the stove and light the fire. The pot needs to be nice and hot for what

I'm about to brew. Everything about this potion is extreme. I'm lucky I have most of the ingredients on hand for it. I'll have to substitute stinging nettle for a scorpion tail, but it'll do.

I grab my packet of peppers out of the fridge. I had them special ordered from South Carolina a few months ago and carefully dried them. Next is the ginseng, tequila, three cubes of ice, and a scorpion tail. The last item takes me a moment to decide.

I run my hand carefully over the drawer of crystals. A pink danburite practically jumps into my hand. It feels bright and ready, it's perfect.

I crush everything separately and set the ingredients in order on the counter. The cauldron is radiating heat. The tequila hits it first and sizzles loudly. I quickly add the rest of the ingredients, the crystal going in last.

I grab my crystal stirring rod and plunge it into the brew. It begins to glow red and grows hot in my hand. Magic beats in my chest as my heart speeds up and I'm breathing like I've just run a marathon. A bright red spark jumps from my chest into the fire under the cauldron, then another, and another, until the fire is burning hotter than it should be able to.

The ingredients dissolve into a black liquid that just barely covers the bottom of the cauldron. Just as it starts to smoke, I lean over the cauldron and take a long, deep breath. The smoke twists up, curling into my nostrils and burning its way down into my lungs. It hurts like hell and my eyes water. I grit my teeth against the urge to scream as energy rushes through me, this brew is strong as hell.

I'm finally able to exhale. I turn off the fire underneath the cauldron as I pant, sweat dripping down my forehead. I've never felt so awake, the next eighteen or so hours should be fun.

I go into the living room and turn on the window unit, cranking the temperature down to sixty-eight degrees. My silky shirt is stuck to me from all the sweating I did between running for my life and brewing a super hot potion. I brace my hands on the window sill and let the cold air pour down shirt. It feels like heaven.

Jessica. Britney. Patrick.

All missing. The girls are dead, which doesn't reassure me about how safe Patrick might be. I have to consider that he has lost control, but the idea of it is ludicrous to me. Patrick is well fed and other than a perverse enjoyment of startling people, a sincerely nice guy. The timing doesn't look great though.

I have no idea if anyone turned up dead before Jessica. I chew at my thumbnail and stare at the detective's card on my dining room table. I hadn't thrown it away after all. He would probably know if there are any other connected disappearances, but I can hardly call him at two am and ask.

Maybelle might know if anyone has disappeared even if she doesn't know about the investigation. I should be able to connect the dots myself. So far it's been neckers. The coven seems to be out on the list of suspects; they're too angry about the potential for bad press. Covens tend to be a lot more subtle about their killing anyhow; the police would never find a body.

My hands are shaking, but with unspent energy instead of lack of adrenaline. I can't talk to Maybelle until seven or eight tomorrow; there's no point pacing my living room worrying about Patrick. I jog back to my workroom. I might as well brew some things I haven't had a reason to brew in ages. Whatever happens next, I want to be armed to the teeth.

I've been sitting outside Maybelle's cafe for twenty minutes when Johnny arrives to open the front door. I've been smelling food baking for almost an hour, and I'm starving.

"The hell you doing out here so early?" He asks as he strolls up. He stops when he's in front of me, his smile dropping into a frown. "Girl, you high on something?"

I smooth my hair down; I'm sweating again. I'd changed clothes, but I think I forgot to brush out my hair.

"Not really, just didn't sleep last night," I say, forcing my face into a smile that has to look even more uncomfortable than it feels.

Johnny shakes his head. "Maybelle don't like you treating yourself like that. You know I don't either. You get in here and have a glass of water, then we're going to have a chat."

He goes over straight back to the kitchen, knowing I'll follow. The cooks nod in greeting, but they're fully focused on getting ready to open. A couple of the waiters are yawning and pulling on their aprons already.

Johnny pauses to pour a glass of water for me and a cup of coffee for himself before continuing back to Maybelle's office. He points at the chair in front of her desk. I sit down and take a long drink of water.

"What did you take?" He asks, his tone steady, as if he's trying to reassure me I can't shock him. If I were to close my eyes, I could imagine Mr. Brunson standing there instead with his cowboy hat, and his thumbs tucked into his gun belt.

"Just a no-sleep potion," I say, bouncing my leg up and down nervously. "It's not a drug, magic or otherwise, it's just a brew that keeps you up for fifteen to twenty hours depending on how strong you make it."

"Now why in the hell would you need to take something like that?"

"I had a run-in with the local coven last night. They were asking me to do something I couldn't do, and I didn't feel safe sleeping last night."

"Why didn't you go to the police?"

I laugh, and it gets away from me. The no-sleep potion can do that, take your emotions to extremes you don't intend. I'm cackling, tears streaming down my face, and Johnny is starting to look concerned.

"I'm sorry," I gasp, wiping away the tears. "It's just that I always forget how human you are, Johnny."

"What's that supposed to mean?" He asks with narrowed eyes, the wrinkles in his forehead deepening.

"Witches and vampires and weres, we have to keep up appearances and look like we are operating under human law, but that's not really how it works. Some witch goes to the police to report a coven is being mean to her? She'd disappear before anyone even had a chance to follow up. Besides, some of the police are part of the coven. My complaint would never make it to anyone that could help and I'd just look weak."

"You know Maybelle would protect you if you needed it."

"I'm doing alright on my own so far. I know I look a little crazy today, but I'm okay, I promise."

He looks skeptical but doesn't push the issue. "Well, you come get breakfast and stay here for today, alright? And you better be ready to talk to Maybelle when she gets in, she should be here around lunchtime."

"Breakfast sounds good, and I need to talk to Maybelle anyhow."

I stop in the employee bathroom and lock the door behind me. My reflection looks at me blearily from the mirror, and I freeze, no wonder Johnny was concerned. Makeup is smeared down my cheeks, and my eyes are bloodshot. My hair is tangled and windblown from leaning into the window unit trying to get cooled off last night.

I rinse my face off in the sink and run my fingers through my hair as well as I can. I still don't look great, but I look more like I'm hungover instead of like I've been on a bender for three days.

The cafe is already half full when I get back to the front. I find a table in the corner and sit down. A waiter, Kevin something, hands me a menu then rushes off again. My stomach growls hungrily. I'd forgotten how much this brew increases my appetite.

I'm ready to order when Kevin gets back, and if he's judging me for how much I order it doesn't show on his face. Good man.

I dig my phone out of my pocket and send a couple of texts to Patrick, just in case, and text Emilio as well. No matter what I find out today from Maybelle, I need to talk to Javier again. With the coven threatening me I want some assurances that the vampires will have my back since I'm sticking my neck out for them.

A shadow falls over my table, and I look up, surprised my food is out already. Detective Jason Martinez stands over me instead. He's wearing a black t-shirt that stretches in a real flattering manner over his biceps and a pair of light wash jeans that I really need to see from the back. I realize I'm staring when he clears his throat, and my eyes jump back up to his face.

"You're up early," he says with a smirk,

I roll my eyes. "I don't always sleep until two in the afternoon, you just caught me on a bad day."

"Why was it a bad day?"

I immediately bristle. They're always on duty, even when they're not. "My sorta boyfriend was sorta fucking someone else."

He purses his lips but doesn't bother apologizing for asking. He just pulls out the chair across from me and sits down. "Anyone sitting here?"

"You apparently," I say with a raised brow.

Kevin shows up right then, three plates of food balanced on a tray. He sets them all down in front of me.

"Oh, you were expecting someone?" Martinez asks, moving to scoot back his chair.

"No," I say before I think better of it. I pull the plates in a little closer, Martinez is eyeing my biscuits and gravy, and I am not sharing.

"Would you like to order anything, sir?" Kevin asks politely. I'm going to have to tip Kevin well.

"Um, sure," Martinez says. "Biscuits and gravy with a side of bacon."

I knew it. I grab my fork and take a quick bite, I'm not waiting for him to get his food.

Kevin hurries away, and Martinez watches me eat my first plate of food in silence.

"So, are you on something?" He asks carefully.

I sigh and roll my eyes, slamming down my fork. "Everyone needs to stop asking me that, it's going to give me a complex."

He waits, like that wasn't really an answer.

"I'm not high," I say as I butter a piece of toast. "Did

you want something in particular? Or just to watch me eat?"

"I didn't really have a plan when I saw you, actually. Watching you eat is pretty mesmerizing so far though," he says with a slow smile that has a heat to it I didn't expect to see from him. Maybe my staring earlier put some thoughts in his head.

His food is delivered, and we eat in silence for a few minutes. I stare at his arms flexing as he cuts through his biscuits and gravy. He stares at me, probably looking down my shirt. I put a large piece of bacon in my mouth, then lick my lips. His eyes follow my tongue, and I have to chew faster to keep from smiling. He grins and looks down at his plate.

Last night I didn't think there was any chance I could ask him about the other missing girl, but the universe has seen fit to deliver him to my table. Maybe it's a sign.

"You heard anything about a girl named Britney going missing? She would have been in Jessica's crowd kind of."

He leans back and wipes his mouth, the flirtatious look in his eye falls away, he almost looks guilty now. "Britney Davidson, twenty-five-year-old white female, her body was found at four am this morning. The preliminary cause of death is blood loss due to a vampire bite."

Shit. That confirms what I suspected. I poke at the last half of my waffle, my appetite is suddenly gone.

"Why did you ask me about her?"

"Last night one of her friends, Dawn, asked if I'd seen her. I hadn't, by the way," I say, flicking my eyes to his to make sure he understands my meaning. "The way Dawn was talking made me think she'd probably disappeared like Jessica."

"Britney was actually killed first. A full week before Jessica as best we can tell. Are you sure you didn't see Britney around a week ago? Anywhere?"

"I'm sure," I say, leaning back and crossing my arms.

"Why are you trying so hard to protect the vampires?" He asks, leaning forward, his brows knit together as he searches my face.

"I'm not trying to protect anybody."

"They prey on these girls, you understand that right? They use them until they end up anemic and then toss them out. They end up addicted to drugs and turning tricks on the street corners, it's not right."

"You really hate vampires, don't you?" I ask, tilting my head to the side.

"No, I don't. I just don't trust them."

I scoff. "Right. You don't hate the monsters that prey on the weak, you just don't trust them."

"Why do you work with them?"

"I already told you, the money."

"You could join the local coven if you need money."

"Are you fucking kidding me?"

"Excuse me?" His brows climb up his forehead, and he tightens his grip on his glass.

"Join the coven? I really thought you were in on it,

that you knew what your partner was up to, but you are actually completely oblivious."

"What are you talking about?"

I lean forward, resting my chin in my hand. "Why don't ask your partner why two people from his coven strong-armed me out of Rudie's last night. Ask why they threatened to kill me and tried to force me to call Novak and pin these murders on the vampires. They asked me to lie. The bitchy one with the red lipstick burned the hell out of my car too."

Martinez is staring at me with narrowed eyes. "I don't believe you."

"That doesn't surprise me," I say leaning back in my chair. "Now, fuck off."

He stands up, his chair sliding back loudly. "If you have information we need, come to the station and talk or next time I'll have to drag you there."

"Oh, onto threats already. I thought you were playing the good cop."

He throws a twenty down on the table then marches out of the restaurant. He falters when he walks past my car. I know it still smells like smoke and the paint on the rear is peeling off and streaked with burn marks.

I have to wait another two hours for Maybelle to show up at the cafe. She frets and repeats everything Johnny already said after she arrived. She doesn't know of anyone else missing and hasn't seen anything out of the ordinary. I don't stay long; I'm not in the mood to have her fluttering around worrying about me right now. She keeps asking questions I don't want to answer.

I sit in my car out front for a few minutes, weighing my options. I could get supplies to make another no-sleep brew, and I might have to, but first I want to talk to Gerard. Maybe he'll be less cryptic today.

Gerard's place looks the same as it always does from the street. I sit in my car for a few minutes regardless, just in case someone was following me, but no one else pulls onto the street. With a sigh, I climb out of my car.

I knock on the door and stumble forward when it swings open then swings right back shut. The latch on the door is busted. I pull out my phone and turn on the flashlight, then pull a vial out of my pocket.

I kick the door, and it swings all the way open this time and stays that way. With one last glance behind me, I step inside. The light from my phone only reaches so far, so I shine it in a wide circle around me. There's the usual trash, but no people as far as I can see.

I walk through the debris slowly, turning around to check behind me every few steps. I feel watched in here.

"Gerard, you here?" I shout. My voice seems to die in the big warehouse.

I finally make it back to his office. The door is wide open. The room is empty.

I pull up to the vampire's house a full hour before they'll

be awake. The nervous energy I've felt all day is fading, and fast. I chug the last of my coffee, but I know it isn't going to stop the crash that's coming.

I climb out of my car and sit on the porch facing the door. The white paint by my hand is peeling slightly. I pick at it absently and lean my head back against the porch railing. I wonder if they find me passed out and sweaty out here after sunset if they'll bring me inside.

I don't have anywhere else to go. I won't put Maybelle at risk by hiding out at her place. I don't think the coven would go after a pillar of the community like her, but covens can be unpredictable. I've always hoped that Javier might offer some measure of protection since I'm an employee, but I've never tested how far that protection goes before.

I send a text to Patrick, even though I know he won't see it; he's probably dead like those girls. I miss that little prankster. He would have brought me inside and made sure I didn't die if he'd been here.

My eyes slip shut against my will. The front door opens, and I force them back open.

"Get in here," Emilio hisses.

I struggle to my feet, my body protesting the sudden movement, and hurry inside. I didn't know they could wake up before the sun had set at all. I had heard rumors about some of the older ones, but Emilio?

He slams the door shut behind me and pushes me towards the stairs. I'm stumbling, my feet not quite wanting to work.

"What's wrong with you?" He asks, irritation plain in his voice.

"Haven't slept in a while, I'm crashing. Stupid brewing and its need for balance." My words are slurred by a yawn that makes my eyes water.

Emilio throws open the door to Javier's room, and half waves half pushes me inside. It's pitch black in a way I didn't think was even possible during the middle of the day.

"Olivia, why do you smell like spice and exhaustion?"

"Morning, Javier. Could you turn on a light? This is kind of creepy."

A lamp flicks on in the corner casting just enough light that I can see around the room now. Javier is still sitting in bed wearing an old-fashioned, white nightshirt.

"Olivia," he prompts when I just stand and stare.

"I took a no-sleep potion, and I'm crashing."

"I heard all of that. Why?"

"The coven threatened me last night. They want me to go to the police and lie and say you've been killing those missing girls."

Javier steps out of bed, his movements smooth and menacing as his mouth curls into a snarl. "And did you?"

"No, you haven't been killing anyone, and I'm not in the habit of lying to the police," I stifle another yawn. "Or doing what a coven tells me."

He's standing in front of me in the time it takes to

blink. My hair flutters around my face from the displaced air.

"Did they hurt you?" He asks, a growl bleeding into his voice.

"No, I didn't give them a chance. My car will need new paint though." He puts a hand on my shoulder to steady me, and I realize I've swayed forward.

"Come sit down." He pulls me to the bed with an arm around my shoulders. My legs are shaking, and my vision is blurring.

"Where is Patrick?"

"Don't worry about him right now," Javier murmurs as he sits me down on the edge of the bed.

"No." I shove at his hands. "Where is he? You know." I hit him in the chest, but it's so weak it's almost a pat. "Is he dead?"

Tears well up in my eyes. I don't want to cry in front of Javier, but the brew is taking its price, and I feel like I'm watching everything from outside my body.

"I don't know where he is Olivia, I need you to find him."

I'm laying on my back, but I don't know how I got here. Javier is sitting next to me looking down at me, his eyes are so black. I think he is touching my face.

"I can't find him. I can't find anybody." The tears are sliding out of my eyes and down my cheeks. I can't stop them. I can't ever prevent anything terrible from happening.

"I have faith in you."

5

It's pitch black, but I'm floating on a cloud. There's something cold here though, it's touching my hair. I blink and try to sit up, then everything comes rushing back to me.

"Fuck," I croak. My mouth feels like it's full of cotton and my throat is sore.

"If you'd like," Javier says with laughter in his voice.

"Lights, Javier," I push his hand away and sit up, glad to find that I'm still wearing all my clothes.

He steps out of bed and turns on the lamp. I have to blink against the light, but at least I can see him now.

"How long did I sleep?"

"All night and all day. The sun just set again." He holds out a glass of water. I take it and chug it and immediately want another. I make a mental note to never use that brew again. I should have come here sooner.

"Mind if I use your bathroom?"

"Not at all, I had Emilio get you a change of clothes. They're on the vanity."

Javier's bathroom is—striking. That's really the best word for it. The floor is black marble, and the walls are blood red. An ornate chandelier hangs from the ceiling casting a dim, but warm light throughout the room. A jacuzzi tub sits underneath a window framed with black, velvet curtains.

The shower is the centerpiece of the whole thing though. There are no doors. The edges curve out of the wall giving way to glass in the front. The left side juts out just a little farther providing a way into the shower. It's big enough to fit about eight people comfortably, just enough for a really decent orgy. There are ten total showerheads, five at the normal height and five at waist level. They are solid gold too.

A change of clothes is waiting for me on the counter as promised. It's not even horrendously immodest either. There's a black shirt that looks like it will be too tight and a pair of black jeans. Emilio even got me some panties, good man. A soft leather jacket with silver rivets on the shoulder is hanging from a towel hook. There's no way I'm wearing that in this heat, but I'll definitely take it.

I turn on the closest showerhead and dump my clothes in a pile on the floor. The water is instantly hot and feels amazing as it washes away the anxious sweat of the last of the forty-eight hours.

Javier has lightly scented shampoo and conditioner that somehow smells like a spring morning. I think I've smelled this on Patrick before, which makes me wonder if Patrick has been in here. I frown, something about Patrick and Javier together seems incestuous.

Patrick would give me such shit for being in this situation today. He always said Javier wanted a taste, but wouldn't ask because I worked for him. I'd have said no even if he had asked, so it was better that he hadn't.

Thinking of Patrick spurs me to move a little faster. I need answers, I should have come to Javier sooner, as soon as I was worried about Patrick. I can only hope that my hesitation hasn't cost Patrick his life.

I look like some kind of vampire groupie once I get the clothes on, especially with my dark hair, which looks black when wet. All I need is some eyeliner and studded collar. I lay the jacket carefully over my arm and walk back out into the bedroom. Javier has changed since I last saw him, he's wearing his usual white shirt, buttoned and tucked in this time, and black slacks. He is reading a book in the armchair by the window.

"Did you have a good shower?"

"It was fine," I say, wanting to cut him off before he gets started with more nonsense. "Where is Patrick?"

"As I said last night, I don't actually know," Javier says, shutting the book. "I want you to find him. I've exhausted all my other options."

"If you can't find him what makes you think I can?"

"You're a very resourceful young woman."

I close my eyes for a moment to keep my frustration from overwhelming me. No one other than my long-dead mother should have any idea what I can do, but this conversation is skirting uncomfortably close to implications that scare me.

"How long has Patrick been missing? He stopped responding to my texts about a week ago."

"It has been eight days since Patrick was last seen. A week before that, Emily went missing."

My heart kicks into overdrive. Emily is one of Javier's newer vampires, which means there are two missing vampires. Two dead girls. If Emily went missing two weeks ago, that would be a week before Britney was most likely killed. More than long enough for a vampire to go from in control, to starving. Most vampires would lose control after just four days without a drop of blood. The question is, who would want to do that? Who would go to the trouble of framing the vampires?

"Anyone else missing?"

"No, and no one is permitted to leave the grounds until this is resolved. Patrick left without permission, he thought he could find Emily on his own. He didn't seem to trust that I was doing everything I could to look for her," Javier throws his book across the room in a sudden movement that makes me take a step back. "I do not want my last words to him to be in anger."

"I don't know how to find Patrick. I think whatever has happened to him is connected to the missing girls the cops have been questioning me about. They were both drained by vampires, but I have no idea where to start."

"I need you to do something," Javier says, his fingers curling over the handles of the armchair. "You are a witch, not some helpless human. Find a way."

"I can't find him, I'm not in a coven, I can't just cast a spell like that."

"Find a way!" Javier shouts. "I have people searching for him, but his scent is gone. Erased. I don't know if he is alive or dead or if someone is hurting him. I have failed him just like I have failed Emily."

He puts his hand over his mouth for a moment, staring at the floor.

"If you do not find your friend, who will? The police will pin the murders on him or me if we go to them, and the coven would rather kill us all than help."

I have that sick feeling in the pit of my stomach again. I know what happens next. I search, and I search, and there is nothing. No clues. No one to help, or even care. I can't go through that again.

I have something now that I didn't have then. It's stupid to consider, but I couldn't live with myself if I didn't do everything possible to find Patrick just because I was scared someone might find out what I could do.

"I'll give you ten thousand dollars if you can find Patrick and get the police to look elsewhere for these murders."

I look up sharply. "I'll do it, but I'm doing it for Patrick. Keep your money."

Some of the tension bleeds from Javier's shoulders, and he nods.

I turn and walk away. It's time to go find my least favorite coven member. I won't be sorry if I accidentally kill him.

Aaron Hall is an arrogant, sadistic, self-obsessed asshole. He is also a talented witch and the only witch within a hundred miles from the Hamilton lineage. The Hamiltons are an old family that emigrated from Britain just before the American Revolution. Their specialty is finding lost things, a weird branch of mental magic that has all but died out.

Finders are almost as sought after as healers. For Aaron to get traded out to a coven in a smaller town with no real power to speak of means, he fucked up in a big way. Whatever the reason, it makes what I need to do so much easier.

He's part of why I came to this town actually, but the coven leader shot me down before I ever had a chance to ask him for help. I figured out for myself that he wouldn't have helped me regardless; after an incident involving one of the neckers right after I moved here.

Aaron, while a terrible person, is also very predictable. Every weekend he ends up at Full Moon

Saloon, the trashy bar at the edge of town with the strip club in the back. He likes girls, feeling like he's the baddest guy in the room, and spending money. Full Moon is more than happy to accommodate all of that. The tricky part will be getting him outside.

The bright blue neon sign set on a pole by the road says 'Full Moo' right now because one of the lights is out. I smirk and park my car behind the bar where there is the least light. It's also fairly close to the back door. I pop the trunk before I get out and pull on the leather jacket, even though it's still hot as balls at eleven pm.

My jacket clinks a little as I move. I'm loaded down with brews just in case I get into some trouble. I grab a little green vial from my pocket and unplug the stopper. Green smoke curls up my nose as I tip it back and swallow the contents. It's minty and sends a chill down my spine that makes me shiver involuntarily.

I shut my eyes for a second and slip back into a version of myself that I don't like to acknowledge ever existed. Desperate. Rash. Stupid. This would have been her stomping grounds if she had lived here. She could work a stripper pole; and did for about six months before things got out of hand and everything changed.

I go around to the front, letting my hips sway as I walk. The windows are all blacked out, but I can hear the bass from outside. The bouncer at the door checks my ID, his face passive as he hands it back and waves me inside.

I push the door open, and I'm almost overwhelmed

by the scent of cigarettes and stale beer. The front area is full of tiny, dirty tables. A long bar stretches the length of the room. The place is pretty empty. There are barely-dressed shot girls getting refills for their trays and a few patrons, but that's it. A curtain separates the bar area from the strip club, red lights flash through the gap like a beacon.

I wind my way through the tables to the curtain and push aside with the edge of my arm. It swings back behind me as I duck inside. There is one large raised platform in the center of the room shaped like a cross. There are poles every six or so feet, at least half have a girl gyrating on them in varying stages of undress.

Men stand around the edges dancing along to the music or watching the girls intently. I walk around a lap dance and almost bump into a man twerking very badly.

Loud laughter draws my attention, and I see Aaron climbing up on the platform with a wad of bills sticking out of his hand as he grinds up on one of the strippers. She bends over and pushes her ass back against him as he drops the money down on her. Two friends are cheering him on. Behind them is a table littered with shot glasses and an empty bottle of tequila.

I plaster a smile on my face and stroll in that direction; forcing myself to look around so it's not obvious I'm here for Aaron. An overweight, balding man leers at me. I'm sure they don't get many women in here that aren't employees.

A shot girl almost walks into me.

"You need anything?" She asks, still walking, like she knows I'll say no.

"Actually yes, can you bring me a bottle of tequila? Something good."

"Hundred dollars baby, you want to open a tab?" She says, holding out her hand.

"Nah, just the tequila will do," I dig out my wallet and count out the money. I'm absolutely sending Javier a bill for this.

I find a table a few feet away from the stage, right in the line of sight for Aaron, and sit down. I drape my arms around the back of my chair and stretch my legs out in front of me, looking for all the world like I'm settling in to watch.

The girl on the pole in front of me is pulling off a bird of paradise in spectacular fashion. I'm surprised they have someone this talented in a smaller town like this. A girl that strong and limber could make a good living in a big city.

Aaron stops grinding on the stripper, and I can see the moment he notices me. He elbows one of his friends and nods towards me. His friend says something to him, but Aaron just keeps staring at me.

The shot girl shows back up with the tequila and a stack of glasses. I hand her another few dollars for a tip and pour myself a drink. I look at Aaron and lift the first shot in a toast, holding his gaze as I toss it back.

He licks his lips and shoves one of his friends when they tug on his arm. I look away, pretending to be interested in the stripper again. He'll either come over here or he won't, the invitation was clear. If he doesn't, I'll just have to catch him in the bathroom or something.

It takes ten minutes and another shot before he walks into my line of vision.

"I know you from somewhere," he says, his eyes traveling from my chest to my feet.

"Tequila?" I pick up the bottle and swing it gently from side to side.

"Sure," he says pulling out the other chair, flipping it around, and sitting down. "What's your name?"

"Olivia." A drop of tequila splashes onto my finger as I pour, I lick it off and hand him his glass.

"Aaron," he says as he takes it, his fingers clumsily brushing against mine.

We drink, and he slams his glass down on the table, sucking at his teeth.

"You're a witch aren't you?"

"Got it in one," I say with a slow smile. "Maybe you can even guess why I'm here tonight."

"Hmm," he says, leaning forward a little further. "A witch, hedgewitch I'm guessing, with no coven in a human strip club. You playing trick or treat?"

"Got a regular Sherlock here. No tricks though only treats." I wink and twirl my finger around the edge of my glass.

"I don't know if you were any good the coven would have snatched you up as soon as you got to town."

"Oh please, the coven doesn't want me because I'm

not willing to kiss their asses or the council's," I roll my eyes. "If they had the balls, we'd be working together. There's no reason something this profitable should be left to the humans."

"Maybe you're right," he hesitates, tapping his fingers against the table. "Maybe if you give me a treat tonight, and it's good, I can get you some more business."

I lean forward. "Maybe that sounds like a deal."

"Do you have it here?" He asks, glancing at my jacket pocket.

I glance over at one of the bouncers. "No, I'm not stupid enough to bring that stuff in here. I'm not looking to get banned."

"Where is it then?" Aaron asks, his hand twitching impatiently.

"Outside, we can go out the back exit over there."

Aaron stands and starts heading toward the door. I have to scramble to catch up, I didn't expect him to be this eager.

He's halfway into the parking lot before he realizes he doesn't know where to go. I catch up and tug on his arm.

"This way," I have to bite my tongue before I add 'dumbass.' I can't go offending the customer.

I open the trunk and pull a black bag towards me and fish out a fat, glass vial. The brew inside is a shimmery silver, I always thought it was pretty.

"Try this, it's a great ride," I hold it out to him.

"You take some first," he says, crossing his arms and

looking down his nose at me like he's caught me out. This shithead obviously knows nothing about brewing.

I uncork it and pour a little out onto my tongue where he can see it. It's cold at first, then warm. It slides down easy and even though I feel absolutely nothing I let my eyes slip shut and shiver.

"Fuck, that's good," I whisper like I can't help it. I open my eyes, wider than normal, and hold it out for him. My breaths are coming in faster just from the adrenaline, it makes it easy to act.

He grabs it and tosses it back like it's a shot. His eyes roll back in his head immediately, and his knees buckle. I catch him awkwardly, he weighs almost twice as much as I do. It's all I can do to tip him towards the trunk and roll his torso in.

He's lying face down with his legs hanging over the edge. I grab the right leg and pull, but his gut is hung up on the latch.

"Should have gotten you to climb in the trunk before I knocked you out," I mutter as I shove his other leg in. He rolls towards the back of the trunk. I hope he'll be easier to get out. I'm ready to be done with this. My heart is racing as what I'm about to do hits me. I haven't done this intentionally in a decade. Last time, just like every life-changing moment so far, it had made everything worse.

I slam the lid of the trunk shut and hurry around to the driver's side of the car. I'm not driving all the way back to my house. I have everything I need with me, and I know just the place to do some risky magic.

The drive back into town makes me feel like I've actually taken some drugs. My eyes flick between the road and the rearview mirror. Someone could have seen me in the parking lot. I could get pulled over, not that they'd have any reason to search the car, but I'm not sure I could play it cool.

I tap my fingers against the steering wheel. Just a few more miles. I pass car after car and can hardly take a breath. The lights fade behind me, and I finally turn down into a less busy area.

The street in front of Gerard's warehouse is deserted as usual. I park my car directly in front of the door and trot back to the trunk. Aaron is still out cold. I lean in and get a good grip under his shoulder, pulling him out with short tugs.

His hair is sticking up my nose as I give one last yank and he comes completely out of the trunk, his legs hitting the ground with a thud. I barely stay standing as his weight threatens to pull me down. One careful backward step at a time, I drag him to the door.

I fumble for the door handle with one hand and lose my grip on Aaron.

"Dammit."

I drop him and get the door open, then grab his arms and drag him into the filth. I kick a few pallets out of the way, then lay him out in the cleared area. I grab the bag with ropes out of the trunk and tie him up as tight as I can. He won't be going anywhere unless I cut the ropes off of him.

I check my watch, it'll be another few minutes before he starts to wake up, so I have time to kill. I check the warehouse again. Gerard is still gone, and other than the ever-present rats, we're the only living beings in the place.

Aaron's leg twitches, his boots scuffing against the floor. I walk over and stand behind him. The first spasm shakes his body so hard his head bounces off the concrete, probably hard enough to leave a sore spot tomorrow. The second spasm is much lighter, and his eyelids flick open. It takes another minute for awareness to filter in.

He looks around with wide eyes, taking in the flashlight sitting on the stool and the surrounding darkness. His breath kicks up, and he struggles against the ropes binding him.

"Where am I? Who's there?" He shouts, his voice going high pitched at the end.

I walk up behind him, and he tries to shimmy over to his other side to face me, but he's tied too tightly.

"It doesn't matter, you won't remember any of this tomorrow."

He goes still. "Olivia?"

I step around into the light and squat beside him.

"What the fuck are you doing to me, you weird bitch?" He screams at me, the veins in his forehead popping out.

"You have something that I need. It's just your bad luck that you happened to be born into the Hamilton family."

He bares his teeth at me like some kind of animal. "I'm not finding shit for you! You can't make me!"

"I know," I say as I reach my hand out and press it against his bare arm.

He flinches, expecting pain or something else I'm sure. When he doesn't feel anything, and I don't make any other movements he stares at me, his eyes flicking between my face and my hand.

"You'll feel it soon. Let me know when it feels like you're about to die."

He starts to struggle again, but all he can do is wiggle and curse. For a witch, he's strangely vulnerable. I know what it's like to live without offensive magic at my fingertips, but I make do with my brews. Aaron is too used to having a coven at his back, but the only protection they really offer is scaring your opponent. As soon as someone is willing to risk the consequences, you're dead.

"Stop it! What are you doing! Stop, stop, stop," he pants. He's starting to feel it for real then. My mother described it as being emptied and turned inside out all at the same time. The pain is secondary to the panicked knowledge that you're losing something. She had thought I was somehow sucking out her soul.

The power is running up my arm and pooling in my chest. It's like I'm slipping into a warm bath after being cold for a long time. A pang of hunger stirs in me, and I wonder why I don't do this more often, but that's an answer in and of itself. Addictions are tricky things.

"Why are you taking it?" Aaron sobs. Big, wet tears are sliding down his cheeks, and he is trembling from head to toe.

"I need to find my friend," I whisper. I don't know why I have this urge to comfort him, especially since he won't remember it, but I hate watching this. It makes me feel like a monster.

"Don't kill me," he pleads. "I'll find them. I'll do it I swear."

"Shhh, I'm not going to kill you."

His face has gone pale, but the trembling is slowing. I'll have to stop soon, but I want to take as much as I can. I need to be able to use the magic to its full potential, I can't afford for it to be gimped like the healing magic.

His mouth parts and he struggles to breathe, drool dripping out of his mouth and pooling on the concrete. I yank my hand away and fall back onto my butt. I know I haven't taken too much, but I pushed it to the limit. He still isn't moving, and I'm afraid to touch him again too soon even though I know I can't accidentally steal his magic.

I leave him to recover, he'll be like this for a while. The new magic is twitchy inside of me, trying to figure out how it fits in and testing its bounds. The healing magic was instinctual after I took it, so I flex my fingers and feel out what I need to do. Finding magic can't be that much different.

I grab the town map from my bag and lay it out on the floor in the light. My fingers trail over the worn paper. I let my eyes slip shut and let the magic take over. It knows who I'm looking for. Certainty rushes through me and out of my fingertips. It feels completely different from the healing magic, it's so much brighter and hotter. I gasp as the knowledge of Patrick's location hits me. The area my finger covers on the map is large, but I know exactly where he is.

Rudie's. He's at the bar.

It doesn't make sense, but I know Patrick is there. My phone rings and I jump. I grab it out of my back pocket, and Emilio's number flashes on the screen.

"Emilio, I found him," I say in lieu of a greeting.

"Good, but we need you here now. Javier has been severely injured."

"What? How?" My heart drops into my stomach. I want to go find Patrick now, but if Javier dies, I don't even want to think of what might happen to the clan. Or me.

"He was attacked while out searching for Patrick, despite the fact that I told him not to leave. It was stupid. Rash. The mistake of a child, not a two-hundred-year-old clan leader."

"I'll be there as soon as I can, but I have a mostly unconscious witch tied up at Gerard's warehouse. I need someone to remove all trace of me from him and dump him in the parking lot at the Full Moon."

"It will be taken care of, now come."

He hangs up, and I shove my phone in my pocket and scramble for the memory erasing brew. I lift Aaron's head off the floor and tip the potion into his mouth, holding his nose shut so he has to swallow. He goes completely limp, and I shove him off my lap and grab my things, throwing them roughly into the bag before running back out to my car.

My hands are shaking as I shove the keys into the ignition and screech down the street. I hope I have enough power to heal Javier. I've never had to heal a vampire before, they heal on their own. Whoever hurt him had to know what they were doing, and it must be bad. I'm not even sure if the healing magic will work if the wound was caused by holy water.

I also need backup if I'm going to go get Patrick. Whoever took him overpowered a vampire, and possibly Javier too.

I drive past Maybelle's, and a siren turns on behind me, the lights flashing in my rearview mirror. I'm the only other car on the road.

"Fuck."

I pull out my license and insurance card, texting Emilio as quickly as I can. Every other word is misspelled, but I don't care. I don't like the timing on this.

The officer shines his flashlight into my car, his hand is already on his gun.

"Olivia Carter?"

"Yes." He hasn't even taken my license, how does he already know my name?

"Ma'am, I need you to step out of the car."

I open the car door slowly, my heart pounding. I wasn't speeding, I hadn't done anything worth getting pulled over for. I step out, and he grabs my arm and shoves me around and into the passenger door of the car, slapping the cuffs onto my wrists. I force myself to stay limp and move with him, not fighting a single movement he takes. My driver's license and insurance have fluttered to the ground.

"Olivia Carter, you're under arrest for the murders of Britney Davidson and Jessica Johnson as well as the abduction of Laurel Ramirez."

What the fuck happened while I was sleeping.

6

The interrogation room is cold, but they, of course, took my jacket. I better get it back, it's growing on me.

I'm still handcuffed, and my legs are chained to the floor as well. I don't know what they think I can do exactly, but they're not taking any chances. Or maybe they're trying to intimidate me. The chains just make them look stupid though.

I've been staring at the mirror-that-isn't-really-a-mirror across from me for about ten minutes. Hopefully, I can catch someone's eye and freak them out, but I'm sure I just look angry. The adrenaline of the arrest wore off, and frustration is taking over. I don't have time for this.

Martinez walks in. His suit is wrinkled, and he has dark circles under his eyes. He tosses a file folder onto the table in front of me and then sits down, taking a sip of coffee from his little styrofoam cup.

"How have you been, Carter? It's been a couple of days since I've seen you."

"I've had better weeks Martinez, but thanks for asking."

"We found some interesting things in your car. Novak isn't sure what most of the brews are. Are you inventing new drugs again?" Martinez's hand tightens around his cup for a moment, and the look he's giving me feels personal. Maybe he feels bad for thinking I'm hot since I'm also a terrible criminal.

"Drugs are so 2013 detective. I brew all sorts of things lately, but they're all legal." Mostly legal. Memory potions are a serious gray area, but there is none of that particular brew left, and what they don't know won't hurt anyone.

"Where have you been since I saw you at the diner?"

"Hmm," I say, tilting my head and pursing my lips. "Sleeping with Javier mostly."

His eyes narrow and his jaw clenches. So he is jealous, interesting.

"For almost twenty-four hours? I guess what they say about vampire stamina is true." His tone is sharp and accusatory. He didn't call me a slut, but it feels like he did.

"I suppose, but when I say sleeping, I mean actually sleeping. I crashed pretty hard that evening and didn't wake up until just after sunset tonight. Javier, the gentleman that he is, made sure I was taken care of."

"So that's what you're going with? Sleeping for twenty-four hours and the only people that can corroborate your alibi are vampires?"

"That's what happened, Martinez. You seem to be under the impression that I'm constantly lying to you when I'm not."

He flips open the folder between us. A picture of Jessica's body sprawled out on the ground is on top. Her face is so, so pale and the vicious bite marks on her neck and thighs are circled in red pen as if I could miss them. He slides that picture to the left revealing a similar picture of Britney, except Britney has started decomposing. It's not a great look for her.

"You've already told me they're dead," I say looking up from the pictures. "Are these pictures just supposed to shock me?"

"Did you know the vampires were going to kill them when you took the girls to them?"

I laugh once, I can't help it. "This is ridiculous."

"Laurel Ramirez, the mayor's daughter, went missing just before sunset today. These girls are already dead, but it's not too late to save Laurel. Where is she? Are the vampires already feeding on her?"

I lean forward, getting as close as the chains will allow. "Martinez, get your head out of your ass and think about who could be doing this. It's not me, and it's not the vampires. And as much as I'd like to pin this on the coven, it's not them either."

"What do you know?"

The door to the interrogation rooms slams open and a woman with steel gray hair pulled back into a neat bun glides in. She's almost six feet tall, with broad shoulders and a square face. Everything about her says she means business.

"You're done questioning my client," she says to Martinez. "Get her out of those cuffs, she's coming with me."

I have no idea who she is, but I lean back and shake my hands at Martinez who is glaring at the woman with a look of open hatred.

The police chief steps in behind the woman, his face red and his jaw tight. "Do as she says Martinez."

Martinez pulls the key out of his pocket and unlocks my hands first. I let the handcuffs fall to the table and resist the urge to rub my wrists even though they ache. He kneels in order to reach the leg cuffs. I lean back and let my eyes trail over him, he looks good down there.

"You won't get away with this," he says as he stands back up, our eyes meeting for a moment.

I follow the woman that is apparently my lawyer out of the police station, relishing in the frustrated eyes that follow me. Novak is standing by the door almost shaking in anger. I flip him the finger as we walk out.

"Please tell me Javier sent you," I say as I jog to catch up with her. She has a long stride.

"Emilio technically, but I do work for Javier," she says as she opens the door to a sleek black car. "Get in, I'll answer questions on the way."

I hurry to comply and slide in on the passenger side. She guns it out of the parking lot.

"What's your name?"

"Lydia Holland. I've been Javier's lawyer almost since I graduated from law school."

"Is Javier still alive?" I have to know.

"Yes, for now. I'm not sure how though." Lydia's voice goes low on the last part, and her hands tighten on the steering wheel.

"So, what are you? A human?" I ask, the question is a little rude, but I don't care right now.

"Yes, Javier has found that useful over the years."

The drive drags, she's driving exactly the speed limit, but it feels so much slower. I tap my fingers against my thigh and try not to sigh out loud. Now is not the time for Lydia to speed despite my impatience.

I throw off my seatbelt as soon as we pull into the driveway and have the door open before the car comes to a stop. The front door swings open as I run up the steps and Emilio leads me through the front of the house to one of the sitting rooms.

Javier is laid out on the rug in the center of the room like a sacrifice. I want to throw up looking at him. There is a stake sticking out of his chest, and he has gaping slices all over his arms interspersed with burns.

"Holy fuck," I whisper.

"Language," Emilio hisses with a glare.

I kneel down beside Javier and put my hands on his face, the only uninjured part of him. He's staring at me silently, and I have to shut my eyes. I can't do this with him watching me like I'm his only hope.

"Patrick is at Rudie's. I don't know why or how or exactly where, but he's there," I say before beginning the healing.

Emilio immediately pulls out his phone and dials someone. I tune out what he's saying and focus on pulling out every bit of healing magic I have. With the new magic swirling around inside of me I feel stronger than normal. I hope it helps.

Javier feels different from a human. The magic burns through him faster and stronger. It's almost like he's flammable and the magic is a spark. I can feel the worst of the wounds slowly closing from the inside out and his skin warming under my hands.

My healing magic is already waning though. I won't be able to heal him completely, not even close. I cling to him, pushing through the fatigue that normally has me stopping. Just a little more. Just a little—

He grabs my arms and shoves me away. I slump back onto the floor, panting. I had pushed a tiny bit farther than I intended. He grabs the stake still buried in his chest, rips it out with a grunt and tosses it across the room. The hole in his chest begins closing slowly.

Another of his vampires, someone I don't recognize, comes into the room with a curvy brunette following closely behind him. Her cheeks are flushed, and she's trembling with excitement. She hurries over to Javier's side and kneels, bending her head to the side to give him easy access to her neck.

Javier sinks his teeth into her neck and the girl moans. I try to look anywhere but at the feeding, however, my eyes keep getting drawn back. Javier is staring at me over her shoulder with a predatory look in his eyes.

"Water?" Lydia has a glass in one hand, the other extended to help me up. I take her hand gratefully and let her pull me to my feet. I take the glass eagerly and gulp it down. The water feels amazing in my throat, I hadn't realized how thirsty I was.

"Thank you."

"No problem, will food help as well?"

"Yes, but I need to talk to Emilio. I need to know how we're going to get Patrick back. He's alive for now, or the magic wouldn't work, but they could be killing him or hurting him. I have to—"

"Olivia," Lydia interrupts. "We can do nothing until Javier finishes feeding, and you need to be at your full strength as well. It will only take a few minutes to eat."

I curl my nails into the palm of my hand. "Fine, but I want to talk to Emilio."

Lydia snaps her fingers at another vampire standing in the corner who immediately runs out of the room, then walks toward the kitchen. I follow with one last glance back at Javier. There is already another human waiting for him to feed on.

Lydia forces an apple on me and watches, hands on hips, until I take a bite. I eat it mechanically because I know that I need it, but I barely taste it.

Emilio sweeps into the room. "The coven refuses to take my call."

I snort. "Too good for everyone else, as usual."

"The wolves, however, are willing to assist," Emilio says, his voice smug.

I look up shocked. "The wolves? They never get involved in anything. Why are they willing to help now?"

"Because I was attacked by humans," Javier says from the doorway. He is standing up straight, but his wounds still aren't fully closed. His skin is flushed from the feeding though, I have no doubt he will recover now. "Humans affiliated with New World Reformation to be exact."

Everyone in the room goes still. NWR is the boogeyman that hides under the bed of every paranormal. A quiet war has been waged against them since before we went public, and it's one that will probably never end. Someone will always hate us, and they will always be there to recruit them and arm them. Paranormals might have power beyond the average human, but our vulnerabilities are just as extreme. Balance, in everything.

"You're sure it was them?" I ask, shoving my hands in my pockets to hide my trembling. I don't want to think about what they're doing to Patrick. They never shy away from hurting people, part of what makes them so scary. They don't just kill, they do everything they can to make us fear them.

"We can't go into this fight with only paranormals. They'll destroy us," I say quietly.

"And who will help us? The police?" Emilio sneers. "Did you forget that they just arrested you and accused you of kidnapping the missing girls?"

"No, but just because it might be difficult to persuade them doesn't mean that we don't need them," I say, stepping forward, my hands clenched into fists.

"Then persuade them, Olivia, if you are so convinced. We will attack Rudie's within the hour, with or without them," Javier says before turning and stalking away.

Emilio glares at me and follows after him.

"I'll make a phone call as well, maybe I can help," Lydia says pulling out her phone.

"Thanks," I say, pulling Martinez's card out of my back pocket and staring at it.

I dial the number before I can second guess what I'm doing. The phone rings once, twice, then three times, then four and I'm almost convinced he just isn't going to answer when I hear a gruff hello.

"Martinez, I have some information for you."

7

"Information," he bites the word out like a curse word. "After I have been asking for days, after an interrogation in which you refused to help me. Now you want to talk?"

"Yes, you want it or not?"

"I'm not sure. Why should I trust anything you say now?"

I bite the inside of my cheek. I knew this wasn't going to be easy.

"Do you want to know why I work for the vampires? The real reason?"

Martinez is silent for just long enough to make me worry. "Sure."

"My mom disappeared when I was sixteen. The coven we were with kicked me out without a second thought, and I ended up with a bad crowd. I was desperate, and I made bad decisions and did bad things, I'm sure you've seen my record. Chief of Police Howard Brunson found me one night when he was off duty and saved my life. He helped me turn things around. The only problem is, paranormals live by a different set of rules than humans. It's hard for anyone to get a job with a felony on their record, but add in being a witch? You're fucked."

I pause, weighing how much about myself I want to tell him. Talking about myself like this feels like I'm stripping off my actual skin.

"The vampires are much more lenient than any of the other paranormals. After Mr. Brunson died, Javier offered me a job. It was humiliating at first and terrifying. They prey on the weak after all. They're monsters that feed on women then, when their blood isn't good anymore, turn them out on the streets to be drug addicts and whores," I say, echoing what Martinez had told me at breakfast. They were stereotypes I had bought into as well.

"Only that wasn't what was happening. There are some girls like that, but they make those choices despite the help Javier offers them. The majority are in college and doing well. They don't allow any of the neckers to do drugs, or anything else illegal. They protect everyone that is associated with them. I still don't like working for them sometimes, but before Javier offered me this job, I was about to start brewing drugs again. Javier saved me. And that's why I'm still working for them. That's why I wouldn't give into the threats and throw them under the bus for these murders."

"What information do you have?" Martinez asks. I just barely stop myself by letting out a big sigh of relief. I still don't have his promise of help.

"Two vampires are missing, they were taken just like the girls, and I suspect being starved into a loss of control. Javier went to look for them again tonight, and they tried to capture him, he was almost killed. New World Reformation are the ones that have been taking the girls and trying to frame the vampires for the murders."

Martinez barks out a laugh. "NWR, that's a pretty bold claim."

"It's the truth," I say angrily.

"Where are these alleged terrorists?"

"Rudie's."

He doesn't respond, but I hear a muffled conversation like he is holding his hand over the phone and talking to someone else.

"What's going on?" I ask.

"So, what is it that you want? The police to raid the bar to prove there are terrorists hiding out there?"

"Yes."

"We can't do that based on your word any more than we could arrest you tonight off one tip. We'll have to get a search warrant."

I bite the inside of my cheek. I won't let Patrick die because the police can't deal with a little red tape.

"Look, just give me an hour or two. I will be able to get something pushed through, the Mayor is all over us to find his daughter," Martinez says with a sigh.

"They could be dead in an hour."

"Look, Carter, I know you're worried, but I need you to be patient. Don't do anything stupid and let me handle this, alright?"

As usual, I can't rely on anyone else to help. Gerard did say that the powers that be wouldn't be getting involved, I guess he was right.

"Olivia, did you hear me? I need you to promise me you won't do anything stupid."

"Sure thing, Martinez." I slip my phone back into my pocket and go to find the others, my stomach churning.

We're standing behind Rudie's in the tree line that's about fifty feet from the parking lot. It's still muggy outside, I don't have any of my brews since someone took them, and Javier is nervous. I've never seen him nervous before.

"You're sure Patrick is in there?" Javier asks quietly.

"Yes." I can feel Patrick still, like a tug in the center of my belly. It's stronger now that I'm so close to him.

Javier straightens and looks over my shoulder. A woman with light brown hair cut in a short bob, wearing nothing more than a sports bra and a pair of men's running shorts, is approaching. She must be the local werewolf Alpha. Even though I've been here over six months, I still haven't met any of the weres, that I know of at least. They keep to themselves from what I've been able to gather.

"Ms. Georgia," Javier says, bending at the waist in a deep bow. "I am honored that you are joining us today to hunt a mutual enemy."

"I couldn't leave all the fun to you, now could I?" She asks with a wide grin that turns her face from stern to youthful in an instant. She looks me up and down. "Who's this?"

"Olivia Carter, hedgewitch." I hold out my hand, and she shakes it firmly.

"Georgia Willis, werewolf and Alpha of this pack," she says, extending her hand behind to the group of about ten weres, a mish-mash of people ranging from what looks like a couple around my age to grizzled old men, all watching us closely.

"It's nice to finally meet you," I say.

She inclines her head in agreement then turns to look at Rudie's. The parking lot is mostly empty, and there are lights on inside still, but there is nothing that would indicate it's housing terrorists. Patrick was probably in there the last time I was here. My stomach twists in anger, and I have to look away.

"I always liked this bar, it's a real bummer we're going to tear it down brick by brick and soak the ground with the blood of every soul contained within it," Georgia says, her eyes bright and her teeth already growing into fangs in her mouth.

"Not to take away from your analogy, but not every soul," I say cautiously. "The mayor's daughter and two vampires should be in there as well. They're on our side."

Javier is holding back laughter, but I had to say something. That would be such an awkward mistake.

She laughs, the sound deep and wild, coming up from her belly. "I will not eat your friends."

Javier and Georgia turn around first, and after a moment I too can hear the rumble of a truck coming down the narrow road that runs past the left side of Rudie's back toward town where we parked.

"It's Lydia," Javier says. "I think she has something for you."

I raise a brow but walk back through the trees to meet her. She steps out of her truck with a small black bag that she lifts in my direction.

"I got what I could, but it wasn't everything," she says as I take the bag from her. It's my brews and my jacket. I set the bag on the ground and crouch next to it as I take inventory.

"Thanks, I wasn't happy about losing any of this." I shrug on the jacket and start loading my pockets with brews. "How on earth did you get it?"

"I just walked into the police station and took it, to be honest," she says with a mischievous smile. "If you look like you belong there, most people don't stop to question you."

I feel like I have a chance of making it out of there alive now. I had felt naked without my brews.

Lydia kicks off her heels and pulls a pair of sneakers out of the truck. She pulls out a gun as well that she tucks into the holster she is wearing under her clothes. She pulls out another pistol as well.

"This one is for you," Lydia says, handing me the gun "It has fifteen rounds in the magazine, and one in the chamber, so don't point it at anyone until you're ready to shoot them."

I take the gun hesitantly. I know how to use it, but it's been a long time since I've held one. "Thank you."

Lydia shrugs. "I know you have your magic, but sometimes you just need to shoot someone."

"You coming in there with us?" I ask as I tuck the gun into my waistband on the left side.

"No, I have to stay alive so I can keep you all out of jail once you are finished rescuing Javier's vampires. I will, however, keep an eye out for anyone trying to run away."

I check my watch, we only have three more hours until sunrise.

"Thanks again Lydia," I say with a nod. She waves my thanks away and I jog back over to Javier and Georgia. I can feel Georgia watching me approach, I can almost feel her hunger to get in there and fight. I understand it.

"Do we have a plan, other than kill everyone?" I ask Javier.

"Don't die," he says with a wink, echoing Gerard's advice.

I roll my eyes and pull out the same potion I had used while kidnapping Aaron. I have three vials left, enough for about nine people. "There isn't enough for everyone, choose three vampires and three wolves," I say, nodding at Javier and Georgia in turn. "It should protect us against anything the NWR has that could knock us out or make us lose control."

Javier waves over three of his vampires without hesitation, while Georgia takes a moment longer, whispering with a man that I think is second in command. He jogs off, then returns with three weres. A slender woman with bright eyes, a burly man, and boy that I suspect is barely over eighteen.

I hand a vial to the slender woman and another to one of Javier's vampires. "Everyone get close to the vial and inhale deeply."

Javier and Georgia step in close, our shoulders touching, and I pop the cork out of the vial. The green smoke pours out, curling up into our nostrils. I hear the weres grumbling that it burns.

"I don't recommend breathing in the fumes from anything else I'll be using tonight."

"Noted," Georgia says, rolling her neck in a circle and flexing her hands.

We start toward Rudie's, Javier on my right and

Georgia on my left. Behind us is the crunch of bone as the werewolves drop to their hands and knees, their skin morphing into fur, and their teeth lengthening into fangs. The transformation is disgusting to watch, but I glance back nonetheless. I never can keep myself from looking.

As soon as the first wolf is changed, he races ahead, fading into the night as he circles around to the other side of Rudie's. The vampires are nowhere to be seen. They're probably already there, I think I see movement on the roof.

As we walk through the parking lot, the lights go out one by one with the sound of shattering glass. Darkness advances before us like a shroud. The lights inside of Rudie's go out all at once and the darkness is complete.

The back door to Rudie's is unguarded, at least on the outside. Georgia crouches in front of it, waiting for Javier to give her the signal. I grab a brew out of my pocket and the glass vial digs into the palm of my hand as I clench my fingers around it. Javier is directly behind me, almost plastered to my back.

Georgia busts through the door with one well-placed kick.

8

Georgia takes one step inside before an explosion flings her back and knocks me in Javier. I'd be flying too if he wasn't there to stop me. My ears are ringing and my night vision is almost completely gone.

I throw a brew inside on reflex and hear a guttural scream as it instantly heats the immediate area by two hundred degrees.

Javier is gone, I don't even feel him move, just the sudden absence as I tip backward. I scramble to my feet as howls erupt around me. A huge, red wolf flies past me through the doorway, followed closely by a black wolf.

There is gunfire behind me and above me. Someone screams and I don't know if it's vampire or human. They're fighting on the roof too, possibly in the parking lot. If they're in the parking lot, then they have us surrounded. They must have known we were coming though I have no idea how.

I run inside. The entire place is smokey, I can't even see the bar from here. There's a man laying on the floor directly in front of the doorway, his skin is blistered and red, and his throat has been torn out. A gas mask hangs half off his face. The burn in the back of my throat tells me that they expected this smoke to knock us out. They're in for a surprise.

A door slams open and I can see a glimpse of movement through the smoke. There's a crack and a net flies out and wraps around Georgia. She howls in pain and jerks as the net crackles and sparks. Two wolves charge into the smoke amid the crack of gunfire.

A vampire drops from the ceiling and is immediately struck in the chest by a bullet. The vampire shrieks, clawing at his shirt. A purple flame licks out of the wound and the room fills with the scent of sulfur.

I dive behind the bar and several more wolves rush inside after me. Wood splinters over my head and a wolf yelps in pain, but one of the guns stop. I army crawl toward where I think the shooters are. There is broken glass and the floor is sticky from spilled alcohol. I'm glad I'm wearing the jacket. I grab two brews from my jacket and fling the first over the bar like a grenade. It shatters and I hope it didn't catch any of the wolves, but it won't keep them down for long. I can hear the panicked gasping for a breath they can't take.

An explosion rattles the glass bottles in front of me and makes my ears ring. Then another, and another. I can't even hear myself breathing at this point, just a faint ringing in my ears. The wolves and vampires must be hurting right now. The explosions are worrying. I can't tell where they're occurring. How many of us are dead now?

The smoke is beginning to clear though, so I peek over the bar and see one of the men firing from the corner. I throw the brew directly at him. It breaks over his black armor and begins to eat through it, glowing bright green. He shouts and slaps at the green fire, but all that does is make his hands burn too. I look away as the fire begins to crawl up his neck, but I can't block out the anguished screams.

Javier is dodging two of the men who have dropped their guns. One is swinging a silver net at him, the other has a long wooden spear sharpened to a point. Georgia is still struggling under the net she was caught in. One of the other wolves tries to pull the net off of her, but yelps in pain as it burns his mouth. There is another wolf dead in front of her. I fumble with the brews in my pocket, trying to find the right one by feel.

Two more men come through the doorway and I twist and fall onto my back, pulling the pistol from my waistband. There's no time to aim. I point and shoot, hitting the one closest to me, but he doesn't go down. He turns his gun on me, his teeth bared and his eyes wide. A wolf hits him from the side, jaws clamping down on the gun and ripping it from his grip.

I jump to my feet to shoot the second man, but a vampire has latched onto him. I finally find the brew I was looking for and throw it at Georgia. The glass shatters over her back and the net begins to melt. She squirms her way out of it and climbs to her feet with an enraged howl.

I leap over the side of the bar and run through the doorway the men had come out of. My gut and my newfound magic are leading me in this direction. We may not be able to win this fight. I have to try to get Patrick while I can.

"Olivia wait!" Javier shouts from behind me. I can't wait, every instinct I have is pressing me to keep going.

The hallway is empty. All I can hear is the wet sound of tearing flesh coming from the bar behind me as my hearing slowly returns. There are only two doors, both closed. The tug in my belly leads me past the first door. I stand in front of the second, hesitating for just a moment before I grab the handle and yank the door open.

Narrow, wooden stairs lead almost straight down. I leave the door open behind me and walk down carefully, both hands on my gun. There is more gunfire overhead, but it's dead silent and dark down here.

The stairs lead down into a tunnel that seems to have been dug right into the ground. It still smells like damp earth down here even though the walls are concrete. There is one dim light dangling from the roof of the tunnel. Patrick is close now, so very close.

The tunnel curves ahead, and there is something is around that turn, I can feel it. I grab a brew with my left hand, my last one, then bring it back up to grip the gun. The ringing in my ears has mostly faded, but I know my hearing still isn't fully back.

I glance behind myself one last time, then peer around the curve in the tunnel. It opens immediately into a circular room that smells like blood and shit. A girl with a blonde pixie cut is dangling from shackles that attach to the ceiling in the center of the room, her hands are purple and swollen. Her head is hanging listlessly and her bruised eyes are shut. She looks like she's still alive though.

A dead vampire, I assume must be Emily, is lying next to the wall behind her. Her face is, for lack of a better word, destroyed. It looks like someone beat it in with a two by four.

I creep forward, one foot in front of the other, my hands shaking slightly as I grip the pistol. I step cautiously into the circular room and Laurel's head shoots up. She sees me and her eyes go wide. She begins screaming and kicking and I lower the gun slightly, but she's looking past me.

The press of a gun to the back of my head is all the warning I get.

"I tried to warn you, Olivia, I had hoped you would listen and let the vampires fight for themselves," Martinez says, his breath tickling my ear. He slides his hand down my arm and rips the pistol from my hand. I manage to hold onto the brew and drop my hand to my side, my fist clenched tightly.

I feel like my heart has fallen out of my chest. Martinez. I hadn't seen that coming at all. If it had been Novak standing here holding a gun to my head, I almost wouldn't have been surprised. Martinez had seemed so earnest.

"Why are you doing this?" I ask, hoping to buy time.

"I believe in the cause," Martinez says. "Walk forward."

He pushes the gun more firmly into my skull and I comply. As I walk further into the room, I see Patrick in my peripheral vision. He is chained to the wall, his arms are stretched taut in each direction and wrapped in silver chains that are burning his skin. His cheeks are gaunt and his eyes are completely red. He's gone feral from the hunger. Chevy is standing next to Patrick, a gun hanging loosely from his hand.

My heart almost stops. Chevy? I had thought he liked me, he had always been so friendly. He was always asking how I was—No. He was always asking about the vampires. Almost every conversation came back to them. A snide comment here or there, asking how business was, seeing if I was having any trouble. He had been fishing for information. Is there no one in this town I can trust?

"This will work just as well. A rabid vampire kills not only the mayor's daughter but his conspirator as well," Chevy says with a grin that is all teeth and spite.

"So that's what you're going with Martinez, killing me too?"

"No, Patrick will kill you, just like he killed those girls."

"You are so full of shit--"

Martinez grabs me by the throat and pulls me flush against him, pressing the gun into my cheek so hard I can feel it grinding against my teeth. "If you had listened, you could have lived. I could have helped you, gotten you a job, maybe even recruited you. You're barely a witch after all. If you stopped using magic, you could live a pure life and be redeemed. You chose this," he says, forcing me to look toward Patrick, whose red eyes are following our every move. His fangs are fully extended and dripping with saliva.

I smell ozone before I hear the crackle of magic.

"Let her go," Novak says as he walks into the room, his gun trained on Martinez. Electrical energy crawls around his free hand, sparking and jumping as he clenches it. Novak's hair is almost standing on end.

"Watch out!" I yell as Chevy raises his gun to shoot Novak.

Novak turns and fires first. A ball of lightning flies towards both Chevy and Martinez. Martinez pushes us both forward out of the way of the magic, then lifts the gun that was pressed into my cheek to shoot Novak.

I grab his arm and slam my elbow back into his jaw. Martinez stumbles back and I throw the brew into his face, dropping down to my knees and covering my head with my arms. The brew explodes in a burst of fire and he shrieks as his skin blisters. A wave of heat passes overhead that I can feel even through my jacket.

More gunfire echoes through the room and I see Novak stumble forward, eyes wide in shock. A red circle is forming on the front of his shirt. He falls to his knees, revealing one of the terrorists behind him. I run for my gun, it's barely ten feet away.

I'm hit from behind and Martinez grabs my hair and jerks me back. I go with the yank, turning and smashing my fist into his jaw. His skin is slick and hot and my fist slides off to the side, taking skin with it, but I can tell it rocks him. I jerk my hair out of his grip and hit him again, forcing him to take a step back.

There's another shot and I feel a hot, sharp pain in my left arm.

"Move again and I'll shoot you in the head!" The man in black shouts from behind me.

Martinez grabs his dropped pistol and shoves me towards Laurel. His eyes are wild with anger and pain. The entire left side of his face is beginning to blister, his eyebrows are gone and his left eye can't seem to open all the way between the burns and the swelling from my elbow strike.

"Grab him," he says pointing at Novak, who's staring at him in both disbelief and hatred.

"You were my partner," Novak says hoarsely as the man in black grabs him under his arms and begins dragging him towards the center of the room.

"You were filth I had to tolerate," Martinez hisses. "Tie them together."

The man in black grabs a thin chain from the side of the room and pushes Novak and me together, back to back. He binds us so tightly together I can hardly breathe.

Laurel is sobbing behind us. I keep looking toward the doorway, hoping to see Georgia or Javier. Surely someone will come for me. Martinez steps up to Laurel and smashes the side of her face with the gun, she goes limp and quiet.

Chevy is bleeding from a wound on his shoulder and his stomach, but he is still standing. Martinez walks over to the door from the tunnel and closes it. The door is solid steel and two heavy bars drop down, reinforcing. My heart sinks into my stomach.

There is another door to the right of Patrick, but it looks like it locks from the other side and is similarly reinforced. I have no idea where it leads. Martinez and the man in black walk toward Chevy.

Novak's head lolls to the side and I grab his wrist, sending my healing magic into him. His wounds are beyond my skill to heal, but maybe I can buy him some time. I can feel him regaining consciousness, but the bleeding isn't slowing fast enough. They must have hit an artery.

Chevy grabs a lever on the wall near Patrick and pulls. The chains fall off and Patrick lunges forward, running straight toward us, concerned only with the smell of blood.

"Patrick, no!" I scream.

Chevy pulls the second lever and a large, round cage falls from the ceiling and slams onto the ground, trapping all four of us inside.

I twist so that Novak is behind me and kick at Patrick as he tries to jump over us and grab Laurel. He turns and hisses at me, no recognition in his face at all. His eyes flick to the wound on my arm and he strikes, his teeth tearing into the muscle. I bite down on the scream and try to yank my arms free, but all I manage to do is bruise myself.

Patrick locks his jaw down tighter and sucks down deep pulls of blood. It burns and aches so much I can hardly stand it.

"You see now, don't you Olivia? They're vicious, soulless, monsters," Martinez says, crouching down by the cage to watch me die.

"The only monster I see here is you," I bite out. Novak is barely hanging onto consciousness, and I don't want to die like this. I grab his limp hand and I begin to pull. The magic rushes into me and I take it greedily. This will speed up his death, but so will letting Patrick eat him.

"Patrick, listen to me," I say, my voice not as steady as I'd like. "I know you're still in there, and I know you're hungry, but--"

Patrick releases my shoulder, and for a brief

moment I think maybe he is listening to me, but he pulls Novak forward, shoving me onto my face, and buries his face in Novak's stomach. I pull on Novak's magic faster, I need more. I can feel Novak dying, he's already lost too much blood. I have to take it all now before it's too late.

I have always pulled slowly before, but this time I reach an invisible fist inside of him and rip out every last bit of magic. Novak dies. I feel his soul leave like a whisper, the one thing I couldn't take.

Electricity crackles around me, my hair lifting around my head. The sharp, bitter smell of ozone overtakes my senses.

Martinez is already running towards the door. "Shoot her!"

The man in black lifts his gun towards me and I push the magic at him, uncontrolled. A jagged bolt of pure energy crackles through the air and hits him in the chest. He falls down face first, his body jerking and spasming.

Chevy shoots wildly in our direction. I throw another bolt of lightning at him. It hits the gun more than him and he shouts in pain as the guns falls to the ground. I feel weak already, I've used too much magic, too fast. There's no stopping now though.

I grit my teeth and hurl another bolt of electricity at Chevy. As it hits him, I realize that Martinez is running out of the other door.

"No!" I shriek, but he pulls the door shut behind him.

I hear the bars slam into place as I struggle uselessly against my bonds again.

He's gone and Novak is dead. Patrick is sucking at the wound on his stomach still, practically bathing in the blood. He's going to hate himself for this, I hope he doesn't remember it. I also hope I can stop him before he kills the rest of us.

I gather the last of my strength and reach back, grabbing Patrick's bony wrist. He jerks when I begin electrocuting him and tries to pull away, but I refuse to let go. I send more magic into him and he grabs my hurt arm with his free hand, digging into the wound. I scream in pain but don't stop.

He bites down on my forearm and I push everything left into him, enough that I'm worried I might kill both of us. His eyes roll back in his head and he finally falls, his teeth ripping my skin on the way out. Blood drips freely from the wound.

I feel like I'm floating now. I'm so tired and everything hurts. I close my eyes to rest, just for a second, when I hear banging on the door I had come in earlier. I think I might have been hearing it for a while.

A strange dent appears on the inside of the door, then another. The door rattles with each impact, the metal straining against the hinges and the frame. Another hit and I realize they aren't dents, they're the opposite. Something is coming through the other side.

There is a loud crack and the concrete around the door begins to give way. Two more hits and the entire door falls down flat in a cloud of dust. Georgia, now in wolf form, and Javier lunge into the room, looking around for anyone else.

"We're alone," I croak out. "Martinez—got away."

Javier runs over to the cage and tries to lift it, but hisses and jerks away when he touches it.

"How do we open it?"

"Lever. Wall."

The cage lifts slowly towards the ceiling and Georgia slides underneath, changing back into her human form as she does. She watches Patrick warily as she yanks apart the chains holding Novak and myself. She pulls me out from underneath Novak. Patrick grunts and holds his meal closer as it shifts, growling irritably at us for disturbing him. He's still not fully conscious. His muscles are spasming randomly.

Javier crouches next to Patrick, smoothing a hand down the side of his face and whispering in his ear. He bites his own wrist and presses a few drops into Patrick's mouth, who latches on eagerly.

Georgia picks up Novak and moves him a short distance away, closing his eyes and folding his hands across his chest respectfully. Laurel is still hanging unconscious behind us, so Georgia moves to get her down next. Javier crouches beside me, his face unreadable.

"Is Patrick okay?" I ask.

"He will be," Javier says, helping me sit up. "Olivia, drink from me. It will help you heal."

"I don't need--"

"You are exhausted magically and physically, please let me help you."

He presses his wrist to my mouth, and I let him. I'm too tired to fight, and some instinct inside of me knows it will help. As soon as the blood hits my tongue, I want to clamp down and suck. I can feel the magic that runs through him, keeping him alive. I could take it, all of it, so easily.

I shove his wrist away. "I'll be fine."

He stares at me, brows pinched together, then finally sighs and helps me stand "You will stay with the clan for tonight at least, we don't know if NWR might try to retaliate. We can't be sure we got them all."

"We didn't get them all. One got away," I say, tears burning at the back of my eyes. I refuse to let them fall. Javier has already seen me cry once.

"Who?"

"Detective Jason Martinez."

The rest of the police are already outside once Javier carries me back upstairs. The mayor is there too, and he sobs as he holds his daughter. She's still unconscious, but the paramedics are saying she'll live.

I get a lot of questions and answer them all the same

way. Detective Novak was able, despite his terrible wounds, to kill two of their men and render Patrick unconscious before he died. I did my best to heal him and keep him alive, but it wasn't enough. The words taste like ash in my mouth, especially since I'm the one that killed him.

They load me into one of the ambulances, one of the wolves goes with me at Javier's insistence. As soon as the painkillers hit my bloodstream, I don't care what they do with me.

———

I manage two hours of sleep after we get back. I still feel dirty, the nurses cleaned most of the blood off of me, but I didn't get a proper shower. Javier had insisted I stay in his room, I didn't bother arguing. Before I had fallen asleep, he had paced the room, asking every few minutes how I was feeling, if I needed anything. I think he wanted the comfort of someone else there as much as I do. He's dead asleep now, curled up under the covers like a little boy. I smooth his hair back and tuck the covers a little tighter around him. I wish I could do the same for Patrick.

The bath fills up quickly with almost too hot water. It feels amazing as I step in. I have to keep my right arm out of the water, but I manage to bathe awkwardly with my left hand. It helps, but I know I still won't be able to sleep.

I change into the fresh pajamas Javier had laid out for me and slip downstairs to the kitchen. Lydia is pouring herself a cup of coffee. She's wearing a fluffy pink robe over a long nightshirt with a picture of a cat on it. She still holds herself like she's in the courtroom though, and the combination is odd.

"Want one?" She asks quietly.

"Yeah, that'd be great."

She grabs another mug and fills it with coffee. I add cream and three scoops of sugar, then follow her out onto the back porch. We sit down on the porch swing and I curl my feet up underneath me.

Javier keeps a really beautiful garden out back. The back of the house looks out down a sloping hill. Javier had a maze of hedges built that covers most of the backyard, but right in front of the porch is a colorful array of flowers that are all pointed toward the sun, drinking up the rays.

"How are you feeling?" Lydia asks as she pushes off the floor with her toe, swinging us backward.

"A little crazy. Worried about Patrick. Scared," I admit.

"Patrick is going to be okay, he'll recover," Lydia says, blowing across her mug before taking a sip.

"But he won't be the same. They hurt him, and even though it was unwillingly, he still killed some people."

"You killed some people too, from what I heard. You both will recover from that. Patrick is resilient, I'm not sure how much you know about his history, but this won't be enough to break him."

I take a drink to avoid answering. I know it won't break him, but I dread seeing him without the twinkle in his eye. "I expected to get questioned by the police again before I left the hospital."

"I was able to get them to wait. You'll have to submit an official statement tomorrow, but I'll be with you, and you'll be rested. There's no reason they can't wait. It's clear what happened, they found all the proof they need."

"How many were killed? Of our people." I can't help but ask, even though my stomach is a tight knot of worry as I wait for the answer.

"Too many. You were right about the slaughter. But less than could have been," she says with a long, slow exhale. "Javier and Georgia are smart. They were able to minimize the casualties."

"What now?" I ask. My hands are shaking, my body thinks I still need to be fighting for my life.

"Just another day, Olivia. There's no point in worrying about tomorrow."

"If you say so," I say with a snort, leaning my head back and shutting my eyes. A breeze blows across the porch and some of the tension leaves my shoulders.

Lydia's phone rings and she pulls it out of the pocket of her robe. She pinches her brows together as she looks at the screen, but answers it anyhow.

"Lydia Holland, how can I help you?"

Lydia pauses, her back straightening as the other person talks. "A representative from the council? Coming here?"

I look up sharply. I was sure the council knew about what had happened here, but it had been handled. Why would they be interfering now?

Lydia turns to me, eyes wide, the phone still pressed to her ear. "What do they want with Olivia?"

Fuck.

Olivia's story continues in PRICE OF MAGIC - She'll have more than one unexpected visitor...Turn the page to read Chapter One.

PRICE OF MAGIC (WITCH'S BITE #2)

F our vampires. Three werewolves. That's how many died that night. Avoidable deaths.

That's all I can think about as I stare at the detective across from me who is waiting for an answer to a question he has already asked twice. He's going through everything that happened for the third time, and it's starting to feel like an interrogation.

"You stated that Detective Alexander Novak was able to kill Chevy before succumbing to his wounds?" he repeats, his brows pinched together as he looks down at me over his glasses like I might be too stupid to understand what he just asked.

"Yes," I answer, again. I have to bite the inside of my cheek to keep from adding a 'for the last fucking time'. My hands clench into tight fists where they are tucked under my arms.

Lydia glances at me and shifts to sit up straighter.

"This interview has gone on long enough. If you have any other questions, you can refer to my client's written statement. After all, she's a victim here, not a suspect in a murder investigation."

I should be. But I'm not stupid enough to say that aloud, though I wonder what they'd do if I did tell them. It's possible they wouldn't even believe me. No one should be able to do what I can do; it's abnormal even for a witch. My mother had made sure I understood from a young age that if anyone ever found out, my life would be over. I'd be killed or used, and I don't like the idea of either.

I want out of this tiny, cold room and out of the police station. There are too many memories that creep up on me in these places.

"Of course, Ms. Holland." Detective Ross says, his mustache bristling as he purses his lips and nods his head. He stands and thanks each of us. His warm hand is a sharp contrast to my frigid one as we shake.

Lydia leads me out of the room. "Do you mind stopping in to say hello to the police chief? He wanted to apologize in person for Martinez."

I sigh but nod. Turning down the chief's goodwill offering would only lead to me looking bitter. I don't want to have to deal with him ever again, but if I do, I'd rather he remember me fondly.

"Let's just make it quick."

I follow Lydia down the narrow, dingy hall. There are office doors every few feet with little brass nameplates. Most of the doors are closed, but a few are open. A woman with a pixie cut is sitting in one office, feet propped up on a chair. She watches as we walk by, eyes narrowed.

The chief's office is at the end of the hall around a corner. The door is shut, but raised voices are clearly audible from where we stand.

"Your coven member interfered in an ongoing investigation. If that witch hadn't gotten involved, an NWR cell would have stayed active in my damn town! For the last time, McGuinness, your coven's petty bullshit feud with the vampires ends now, or I won't have another witch in this department. I'll report you to both councils if I have to."

McGuinness' response is muffled by the door.

Lydia and I share a look. Her brows are raised, and she's smirking. I can't help smiling as well. I've waited my entire life to hear a coven leader get dressed down like this, and it's just as satisfying as I imagined.

McGuinness went out of his way to make sure I understood I would not be joining his coven as soon as I moved into town. It had almost been enough to run me off before my stubbornness kicked in.

The door flies open, and a red-faced man in a suit that barely stretches across his chest comes barreling out, almost running right into me.

At first he just looks annoyed, but then he recognizes me, and his face turns even redder. He bares his teeth at me, brows furrowed and nostrils flaring. He steps forward, his fingers twitching like he's thinking of casting a spell. I uncross my arms and take a step toward him, holding his gaze. He can fucking try, but it'll be the last thing he does.

Novak's magic is buzzing through me. The coven leader has no idea I have it. I want to fry him to a crisp. I feel a spark on the tip of my finger, then Lydia is jerking me back and getting between us. Sound filters back in, and I realize the chief is shouting at McGuinness again, ordering him out.

McGuinness brushes past Lydia and stomps down the hall without a backward glance, taking the smell of fire with him. My breath is coming uncomfortably fast. The Chief and Lydia are both staring at me, the latter with pinched brows and lips pressed tightly together.

"Olivia, are you all right?" Lydia asks.

"I'm fine," I say, clearing my throat and straightening my jacket.

The chief holds out his hand. "Chief of Police Samuel Timmons. It's good to meet you in person, Ms. Carter."

I shake his hand. "Likewise."

"I intended to apologize for the mishandling of the investigation, but it appears I will also need to apologize for the behavior you just witnessed. I would like to make it clear that I will not be party to the coven's obvious prejudice."

"I appreciate that," I say with a tight smile. "Not your fault he's an ass."

"Do you have a moment to sit down?" Timmons asks, waving back toward his office.

"Sure," I agree.

Lydia tugs my arm to get me to follow Timmons into his office.

His desk is oversized and cluttered. There's a bookshelf behind him filled with awards and pictures of his family, but no books.

"Now, we are still looking for Jason Martinez. We don't have any information yet, which isn't surprising considering his connections. I've been in contact with JHAPI and the Vampire Council. From what I hear, there will be a representative from the Vampire Council coming to town to assist JHAPI with the search if he can."

Joint Human and Paranormal Intelligence are involved? They must be serious. That particular organization hasn't actually been around that long, only six years if I remember right. It was formed after the NWR became a more public problem. It was the first cooperative human and paranormal task force created, and it was a surprising success. The councils are always vying for influence over it, of course, but JHAPI has been successful in slowing down the NWR over the years despite that.

"Please keep us updated, Chief Timmons. We, of course, will continue to help in any way we can," Lydia says politely.

Timmons pulls two cards out of his desk and scribbles a number on the back of each. "My personal cell number is on the back. Don't hesitate to contact me if you need anything or have any information."

I stand and tuck the card into my jacket. "Thanks."

"We'll be in touch," Lydia says.

I walk out before he can think of anything else to discuss. I'm halfway down the hall before Lydia makes it out of his office. I can hear her hurrying after me, but I don't slow down until I'm in the parking lot.

I lean back against my car and cross my arms. There's a crisp coolness in the air that wasn't there yesterday. The first hint of fall always comes as a surprise to me. Summer seems endless until I walk outside and it smells different, and a breeze raises goosebumps on my arms.

She comes to a stop in front of me. "Will you reconsider staying at the clanhouse for the rest of the week?"

"No, I need to feed my cat and catch up on brewing," I say as I pull my keys out. "I also don't want another night of Javier hovering over me like some kind of creepy mother hen."

Lydia sighs, but her lips curl up into a smile. She had laughed at me this afternoon after I finally woke up when I had complained. "He means well."

"I know." I gnaw at the inside of my cheek. "How is Patrick?"

"He is not himself yet. Which is why Javier is being so ridiculous. Patrick won't let him hover either."

I roll my eyes. That's the most I've gotten out of her since yesterday morning, and it's not enough.

"You're being vague. Not himself," I mock, throwing up sarcastic finger quotes. "Javier wouldn't let me see him, so something is obviously wrong. Just tell me."

Lydia huffs and shakes her head. "Javier didn't want you to worry, but I suppose that's impossible. Patrick is angry. He has had several outbursts. He almost hurt one of the neckers and did not appreciate the manner in which Javier stopped him. They've been arguing like cats and dogs."

"I want to talk to him."

"Javier has said no visitors since the incident with the necker. He's even having his blood delivered in a cup."

I grimace at the visual. "That's only going to piss Patrick off more. Is he really that out of control?"

"I don't know." Lydia clasps her hands in front her, thumb tapping restlessly against the back of her hand.

I need to see Patrick, but I can't deny the little shiver of fear that accompanies the thought. Especially if he isn't fully back in control. The rational mind has a hard time reconciling that a friend could try to kill you and it is not their fault.

"I'm going to come see him soon, whether Javier likes it or not."

"Just give him one more night, Olivia. I wouldn't ask

you that if I didn't think it was best for Patrick too. He's struggling for control right now."

I nod. Lydia's honesty is what I need right now. "Any news on when the council representative is coming? Or why they want to see me specifically?"

"Nothing yet," Lydia sighs. "They won't tell me who they're sending, or when. Javier is preparing for the visit as best he can."

"Do you think I'm in some kind of trouble?"

Lydia taps a finger against her chin, considering.

"Having the council's attention is never a good thing, but I don't think you are in trouble for something you did," she says. "You'll have to be careful, and I know this goes against all your instincts, but please be polite to the representative they send."

I roll my eyes. "I'll be polite if they're polite."

"Olivia, this will not be someone like any of the vampires you've met. They'll be old, and strong, and possibly not willing to deal with any attitude."

"I'll figure it out. Just keep me updated, all right?" I say, crossing my arms. She has no faith in me. I'm not a six-year-old. I can be polite if I need to.

"I'll keep you updated. Oh, that reminds me. Will you still be able to come by for the regular checkups this week?"

"Yes." The return to routine sounds like a nice distraction.

Lydia squeezes my arm gently. "Stay safe, and stay in touch, all right?"

"Sure thing," I say as I slip into my car.

Lydia watches me drive off, her lips one thin line. I must seem worse off than I thought if she's worrying this much.

We spent almost three hours at the police station. The sun is setting now, and since it's a cloudy night, it's magnificent. I roll the windows down and dance my fingers in the brisk wind. Patrick is alive. I'm alive. We won. That should be enough to get this sick feeling out of my stomach.

Yet, all I can think about is how it felt when Novak died. I wasn't even sure it was possible to kill someone just by taking their magic.

I smack the power button on the radio. I have to stop thinking about this; it's not healthy. Avoidance is a much better option. Tequila might work too, but I don't think I have any left.

I sing along with the radio as I drive. Classic rock, then some generic pop when commercials come on. I'm ready to be home. If I can just bury myself in normalcy, maybe I can get this knot of anger in my chest to loosen.

Martinez's face, the skin twisted and burned on one side, seems to be all I can see every time I shut my eyes. That or Laurel Ramirez hanging from the ceiling like a side of meat. Or Patrick with empty eyes and spit dripping from his chin, nothing left but hunger.

I turn down my driveway, finally, and I'm relieved to see everything is as I left it. The kitchen light is on, and the porch is lit up. I park, grab all my things, and hurry to the front door, keys ready. As soon as I open the door, Mr. Muffins is twining between my legs, meowing loudly.

"I know, I know, I'm sorry," I say as I trip my way inside.

She bites my ankle through my pants.

"Ow! Give me a damn second." I dump my keys, gun, and jacket on the table and go to the laundry room to refill her water and food, only to find they're both still half-filled. I turn around and glare at her. She's sitting in the middle of the kitchen, licking her paw.

"Seriously? All that, and you aren't even starving?"

She meows and stalks over to the fridge.

"I see how it is. You miss one day of treats and turn feral," I grumble as I get a can of wet food out of the fridge. Mr. Muffins is aggressively spoiled, and I only have myself to blame.

The can opener is still in the sink from the last time I fed her. I open the can as she paces back and forth behind me.

"Here you go, Princess Butthead," I say as I drop the can on the floor and ruffle the fur on her head. She buries her face in the food and ignores me.

Everything is where I left it, including the pile of dirty clothes in the bathroom and the mess in the work-room. I don't want to deal with any of it. It'll still be here tomorrow anyhow.

There's a knock on the door, and I jump, my heart kicking into overdrive. No one ever visits me. If Javier were having someone dropped off to be healed, I would have gotten a text.

I walk as quietly as I can to the table and grab the gun. I should have just gotten Mr. Muffins and stayed at the clanhouse.

"Olivia?" the person shouts through the door.

I'd know that voice anywhere. It's Patrick.

A PLOT BUNNY

When I started writing Borrowed Magic...I was supposed to be writing something else. I had just finished revising a Book 1 in a wildly different series. I had an outline for Book 2 in that series, and a goal for when I needed to finish writing it.

Then a plot bunny arrived. It was aggressive. I was weak-willed. I have no regrets.

I wrote the first draft in less than a month, which was crazy to me! The last book had taken years to write. Something about Olivia filled me with excitement.

Book 1 Spoilers Below (just in case you skipped to the end) - You have been warned.

Martinez was originally intended to be her love

interest throughout the series. Believe me, I was surprised to discover that he was, in fact, the bad guy. But I went with it, and I'm glad I did. I hope you enjoyed it too :)

MESSAGE TO THE READER

Thank you so much for buying my book. I really hope you have enjoyed the story as much as I did writing it. Being an author is not an easy task, so your support means a lot to me. I do my best to make sure books come out error free.

However, I am the worst with commas. They are my nemesis. I deeply apologize if my comma usage bothered you. Going forward, I am hiring a professional editor to review the books before publication. Eventually, I will be able to have previously published books edited as well. If you found any errors, please feel free to reach out to me so I can correct them!

If you loved this book, the best way to find out about new releases and updates is to join my Facebook group, The Foxehole. I love seeing new faces in there and getting to interact with my readers :D It makes writing easier, and my day better!

Amazon does a very poor job about notifying readers of new book releases. Joining the group can be an alternative to newsletters if you feel your inbox is getting a little crowded. Both options are linked below :)

Facebook Group:
https://www.facebook.com/groups/Thefoxehole
Newsletter:
https://stephaniefoxe.com/newsletter-wb/
Goodreads:
http://goodreads.com/Stephanie_Foxe

P.S. Who's your favorite character? Let me know in the Facebook group.

MAKE A DIFFERENCE

Reviews are very important, and sometimes hard for an independently published author to get. A big publisher has a massive advertising budget and can send out hundreds of review copies.

I, however, am lucky to have loyal and enthusiastic readers. And I think that's much more valuable.

Leaving an honest review helps me tremendously. It shows other readers why they should give me a try.

If you've enjoyed reading this book, I would appreciate, very much, if you took the time to leave a review. Whether you write one sentence, or three paragraphs, it's equally helpful.

Thank you :)

To review the book simply go to the website below.

https://readerlinks.com/mybooks/765/1/1237

Misfit Pack is the first book in a new series by Stephanie Foxe –

A redhead with a drawl, a lawyer with pink hair, and a homeless seventeen year old have no business forming a pack.

In a world where magic is commonplace, and your neighbor is just as likely to be an elf as a troll, three humans are unwillingly changed into werewolves.

Unprepared and unwanted.

The pack may have chosen Amber as their Alpha, but that's

not a title she is supposed to have. In order to be legally recognized as an Alpha she must pass the Trials, and it won't be easy. If she fails, her pack will be disbanded and forced into a halfway house for bitten werewolves, aka The System.

But the pack needs a sponsor in order to even enter the Trials.

With everything to lose, the brand new pack must learn to work together before it's too late.

www.stephaniefoxe.com

Printed by Amazon Italia Logistica S.r.l.
Torrazza Piemonte (TO), Italy

10288500R00084